STEALING TIME

STEALING TIME

Anne Dublin

DUNDURN
TORONTO

Editor: Laura Harris
Design: Courtney Horner
Printer: Webcom

Library and Archives Canada Cataloguing in Publication

Dublin, Anne, author
    Stealing time : a Jonah Wiley adventure / Anne Dublin.

Issued in print and electronic formats.
ISBN 978-1-4597-0973-7

    I. Title.

PS8557.U233S74 2014   jC813'.6   C2013-907393-0
                                               C2013-907394-9

1 2 3 4 5   18 17 16 15 14

We acknowledge the support of the Canada Council for the Arts and the Ontario Arts Council for our publishing program. We also acknowledge the financial support of the Government of Canada through the Canada Book Fund and Livres Canada Books, and the Government of Ontario through the Ontario Book Publishing Tax Credit and the Ontario Media Development Corporation.

Care has been taken to trace the ownership of copyright material used in this book. The author and the publisher welcome any information enabling them to rectify any references or credits in subsequent editions.

J. Kirk Howard, President

The publisher is not responsible for websites or their content unless they are owned by the publisher.

Printed and bound in Canada.

The author gratefully acknowledges the support of the City of Toronto through the Toronto Arts Council and the Ontario Arts Council.

Visit us at
Dundurn.com | @dundurnpress | Facebook.com/dundurnpress | Pinterest.com/dundurnpress

Dundurn	Gazelle Book Services Limited	Dundurn
3 Church Street, Suite 500	White Cross Mills	2250 Military Road
Toronto, Ontario, Canada	High Town, Lancaster, England	Tonawanda, NY
M5E 1M2	LA1 4XS	U.S.A. 14150

For Ephraim and Toby

"The past is the stuff that time is made of."
JORGE LUIS BORGES, "THE WAIT," (1950)

1

PRESENT TIME

"I won't go and you can't make me!" shouted Jonah Wiley.

"You've got to," said Mrs. Wiley. "You're supposed to visit your dad every second weekend. And now that they're back from their honeymoon —"

"I don't care." Jonah glared at his mother. "I'm *not* going."

Mrs. Wiley's shoulders sagged. "We've already talked about this. You know I have to go to my conference this weekend."

"Yeah. You talked and I listened." Jonah kicked the table leg rhythmically. "I hate going over there." He crossed his arms. "I don't want to see Dad and his new wife and her goofy kid."

"But they're nice to you." Mrs. Wiley furrowed her forehead. "Aren't they?"

"Yeah. *Too* nice," said Jonah.

"What do you mean?"

"It's like ... everyone's trying too hard to get along."

"I see." Mrs. Wiley pursed her lips. "But you know I can't make other arrangements now."

"Fine," said Jonah. "Then I'll stay here by myself."

"No way!" Mrs. Wiley reached out to brush the hair off Jonah's forehead but he jerked his head away.

"I'm twelve years old. I'm not a baby!"

"You can't stay here alone." Mrs. Wiley crossed her arms in her "no nonsense" pose. "And that's that."

"You can't make me go!" Jonah yelled.

"Jonah!"

He stomped up the stairs, stormed into his room, and slammed the door. He threw himself onto his bed and stared up at the ceiling.

Jonah usually loved to be in his room. He had a collection of clocks and watches and kept them in a special cupboard his dad had built for him. The sound of their ticking and chiming and whirring made him feel secure — as if there were a rhythm and order in the world. But since his parents' divorce, there hadn't been much of that.

His bookshelves were crammed with books and magazines about the history of timekeeping. Jonah loved to repair old timepieces that he found at antique shows or garage sales. He would take them apart, placing each tiny part in exact order on his desk. He'd lose track of time when he was busy with a watch or clock.

But now, even his clocks and watches gave him no comfort. Everything felt wrong. His mom spent long hours at work; his dad had remarried and was busy with his new wife, Pam, and her son, Toby. Nobody had time for him anymore.

Mrs. Wiley knocked on his door. "Jonah, can I come in?"

Jonah didn't answer.

"Jonah?"

"All right," he mumbled. His mom padded into his room in her worn-out moccasins. Her grey sweatshirt showed stains from the spaghetti sauce she'd made for supper. Her salt-and-pepper hair was disheveled; her hazel eyes were damp, as if she'd been crying. Jonah hated to see his mom like that, especially when he knew it was his fault.

Mrs. Wiley sat down on his bed. "Jonah, I know it's been hard for you since your dad and I got divorced." Jonah didn't say anything.

"And I know it's been harder still since he got remarried last month." Jonah felt a lump in his throat.

"Let's get through this weekend. I promise we'll work something out about your visits."

"Don't make a promise you can't keep." Jonah sat up. "I know about lawyers. I'm not a kid anymore."

"All right," Mrs. Wiley sighed. "I won't promise. But I *will* try." She stood up. "Will you get ready? I have to drive you over there in half an hour."

"Okay. I don't like it, but I'll do it this time."

"That's the way!" Jonah could hear the relief in his mother's voice. "And don't forget your toothbrush!"

When Jonah arrived at his dad's new place, he could see the flickering TV through the living room window. *They're probably all huddled around the TV set, like one big happy family,* he thought. He swallowed hard. *It should have been me and Mom and Dad — not some other woman and kid living with Dad. And now I've got to spend the whole weekend with them.*

Mr. Wiley opened the door. Jonah felt like falling into his arms and begging him to come home. But he knew that was crazy. His dad was home, only not the home where Jonah wanted him to be.

"Hi, Greg," said his mom.

"Hi," said Jonah's dad. He stepped aside. "Come in."

"No, I won't. I mean, I can't. I've got to go." She handed him a piece of paper. "Here's the information about where I'll be this weekend."

Mr. Wiley peered at the piece of paper. "Thanks," he said, stuffing it into his pants pocket. There was an awkward silence.

"I guess I'd better be going." Mrs. Wiley gave Jonah a peck on the cheek and a quick hug. "You'll be fine," she whispered in his ear. "Try to get along."

That's easy for you to say, thought Jonah. *You don't have to stay here with these people. You can go to your fancy conference and forget all about me.*

"Come in, Jonah," said his dad. "Don't be a stranger." He led Jonah into the living room. *The house looks like a model home,* Jonah thought. *Every piece of furniture matches. It doesn't feel like a house where people live, but a place to show off Pam's perfect taste.*

"Hi, Jonah," said Pam. "How are you?"

Jonah shrugged. *I know I'm being rude, but I can't help it.*

"Hi, Jonah," said Toby. "Want to watch TV?"

"Dad, can I go to the *guest* room?"

Jonah saw the hurt look in his dad's eyes. "All right. Should I go with you?"

"No thanks. I know the way."

Jonah grabbed his bag and dragged it up to the third floor. He liked the room with its sloping rafters and brass bed covered with a handmade quilt. *It's far from the other bedrooms and that's fine with me*, he thought. *I don't want to be part of this family anyway.*

Not bothering to unpack, Jonah plopped down on the bed. He listened to music and soon drifted off to sleep.

The sun was streaming through the window when Jonah opened his eyes. He could smell the autumn crispness in the air.

I wish I were home, he thought. *I would help Mom rake the leaves. Then we'd sit around and drink hot cocoa.... No. She's not home. I'm stuck in this place, with no one to talk to and nothing to do.*

"Jonah? Are you awake?" Mr. Wiley called from the other side of the door. "Jonah?"

"I am now."

"Sorry," mumbled his dad. "Want to come down for breakfast?" Jonah imagined him standing there, hesitant to walk in. "Pam's making her extra-special, ultra-light pancakes."

Suddenly Jonah realized how hungry he was. "I'll be down in a minute."

"All right, but don't take too long." Jonah heard his dad walk down the stairs. *For a big man, he's pretty light on his feet.*

Jonah rolled out of bed and made his way to the bathroom. He washed his face, brushed his teeth, changed into clean clothes, and combed his hair. The smell of buttermilk pancakes made his mouth water as he walked into the kitchen.

"Hi, Jonah," Pam said. She wore an apron with yellow daisies that matched the kitchen walls. She held a spatula in her hand. "Pancakes coming right up."

Jonah sat down and looked around. Outside, the sun was shining and birds were singing. He was about to eat a delicious breakfast. And he felt miserable.

"Hi, Jonah," said Toby, looking up from his drawing.

"Hi," said Jonah. *What's this ten-year-old kid to me? No brother of mine, that's for sure.*

Pam turned off the stove, placed the platter of pancakes on the table, and sat down. "Who will say grace?"

"I will!" said Toby. He closed his eyes. "Thank you, God, for buttermilk pancakes and maple syrup and orange juice and for … my new brother!"

Jonah stared at Toby. *I don't want to be anyone's new brother — least of all this kid's. Even if he does look like me, with his dark hair and eyes. Besides, he's always drawing stupid pictures everywhere he goes.*

"Here, Jonah, have some pancakes," said Mr. Wiley.

Jonah helped himself to three pancakes and doused them with butter and maple syrup. He wolfed them down and then stood up from the table. "I'm going to my room."

"But Jonah," said Mr. Wiley. "I thought we were going to the antiques show at the mall this morning."

"Maybe later."

Jonah stomped up the stairs. *They're probably talking about me,* he thought. *About how I'm being unfriendly; about how I'm not trying to adjust. Well, I don't* want *to adjust! I want things to be exactly how they used to be.*

A few minutes later, Mr. Wiley knocked on the door. "Jonah, are you going to stay in your room all weekend?"

"Maybe. What's it to you?" *I know I'm being rude again, but I can't help it.*

"Can I come in?"

"I guess so."

His dad walked in and the room suddenly seemed smaller. He stood over Jonah as if he were the giant who had discovered Jack at the top of the beanstalk.

Mr. Wiley hesitated and then sat down on the bed. "What's up, Jonah?"

"Nothing."

His dad paused for a moment. "Is it ... my new marriage? Is that what's bothering you?"

Jonah glared at his dad. "What do *you* think?"

"Maybe when you're older, you'll understand."

"That's what grownups always say!" said Jonah.

"I'm old enough now. And I *do* understand." Jonah began to cry and wiped his cheeks with his sleeve. "You're never coming home again, are you?"

His dad reached out but Jonah drew back. "This is my home now, Jonah. I'm sorry that upsets you."

"'Upsets' me? Are you kidding? *Upset* isn't the word!"

Mr. Wiley stood up. "I guess I'd better go." His hand was on the doorknob. "I'll talk to you later."

"Yeah, right." Jonah stared at the closing door. He turned on his music and tried to block out the world.

2

PRESENT TIME

It didn't work, of course.

An hour later, Mr. Wiley was knocking on the door again. "Jonah?"

"Come in."

Jonah's dad stood at the door. *As if he wants to make a fast getaway,* Jonah thought. "So, are you ready to face the world yet?"

"Maybe."

"Why don't we go to that antiques show today? Maybe we'll find a special watch for you."

"Well ..."

"Come on, Jonah." His dad smiled and sat down on the bed. "I know how you love clocks and watches."

"Yeah, well." Jonah almost smiled back. "I remember how Grandpa gave you his pocket watch just before he died."

"It had a lot of memories for him. The wild stories he would tell ..." Mr. Wiley had a faraway look in his eyes. "I've always loved that watch."

"Me too."

"I'm planning to give it to you when you're older, you know."

"What about Toby?" The words stuck in Jonah's throat. "Isn't he your son now, too?"

"I'll give him a box of watercolours," said Mr. Wiley, smiling.

"I miss Grandpa."

"Me too."

"Dad?"

"Yes?"

"Did you ever wish you could stop time? Or slow it down? Or even make it go backwards?"

"I guess so," said Mr. Wiley. "Everyone wishes that at one time or another."

"Does Toby have to come with us today?"

"Pam's taking him to the art gallery. It'll be just the two of us."

Jonah paused a moment before responding. "Sorry, Dad." He lay down on the bed. "I want to be alone for a while."

"Are you sure?"

"Yeah." Jonah tried to hold back a smile. "Anyway, now you can go to the art gallery, too."

Mr. Wiley winked at his son. "Gee, thanks."

At last it was quiet in the house. Everyone had gone. The more Jonah thought about the past year, the more miserable he felt. Sure, he knew his mom and dad loved him. But it wasn't enough. He felt as if he were living in a world of shifting sand. He yearned to do something, anything, to make things change back the way they had been.

Only a year ago, his parents had been together. Jonah knew they hadn't been getting along; that under the surface, his parents were miserable. At night, when they thought he was asleep, they would have big arguments.

Grandpa Wiley had had a way of smoothing things out between his parents. But now he was gone. Cancer had killed him quickly and everything had fallen apart after that.

Dad had moved into an apartment. Then he had met Pam and before Jonah could catch his breath, they'd gotten married.

I want to look at Grandpa Wiley's watch, Jonah thought. He knew exactly where it was — in the special holder in the dining room hutch. Jonah tiptoed down the two flights of stairs. Even though he was alone, he couldn't shake the feeling that someone was watching him.

The watch was tucked in a corner behind the glass door. Jonah lifted the cover of the holder off and took the watch off its little hook. *It's the most beautiful pocket watch in the world.* The golden case gleamed like something alive. Intricate designs had been carved around the edge. A long gold chain was threaded through a loop at the top of the case.

Jonah pushed the knob at the top of the case. Black Roman numerals were etched on the face of the watch. There was only one hand on the watch — the hour hand. The watch was over three hundred years old — it was treasured by his father and had been by his father before him; an object beyond price.

Grandpa Wiley said he'd won the watch in a game of cards with a man he'd met in Bremen, Germany. He always said he was going to donate it to a museum. But then he got sick and everything had ended — his plans, his stories, his life.

Jonah gazed at the watch, sighed, and closed the case with a loud click. He stroked the golden case. *Dad told me it will be mine eventually. Why not take it now?* Jonah thought. *Besides, he's so busy with his new family that he won't even notice it's gone. I'll take it home. It'll remind me of Grandpa Wiley and how things used to be.*

The watch was drawing Jonah in, pulling him with a wanting he had never known before. He took a big breath. His fingers closed around the watch and he shoved it into his pocket.

His heart pounding in his ears, Jonah hurried back up the stairs to his room. *I shouldn't have taken the watch. I know it was wrong. But I don't care.*

Later that afternoon, Jonah took the watch out from its hiding place in his dresser. He turned the case over and read the words engraved on the back of the case:

Time as he grows old
teaches many lessons.

– Aeschylus

Just then, Toby exploded into the room. "Mom wants to know —"

"What do *you* want?" Jonah growled. He thrust the watch behind his back.

"Sorry." Toby crossed the room and peeked over Jonah's shoulder. "Hey, what's that? Is that —?"

"Nothing. Go away!"

"Let me see!"

"No!" Jonah moved his hand away but Toby grabbed the watch.

"Hey. This is really something." Toby hopped out of reach.

"Give it back to me! It's mine!" shouted Jonah.

"Where did you get it?"

"Dad gave it to me," Jonah said.

Toby looked puzzled. "He did? But I thought —"

"Give it back, I said!" Jonah tried to grab the watch but Toby yanked his hand away.

"Can I see how it works?" said Toby. "Then I'll give it back."

"No!"

Toby pushed the knob at the top of the watch. The case opened with a loud click. "Cool. But why is there only one hand?"

"That's the way they made watches in the olden days," said Jonah. "They didn't have exact ways of measuring time like we do. They —"

"You sound like a teacher," said Toby. "I'm going to wind it."

"Don't! You'll break it!"

"No I won't." Toby turned the knob at the top of the watch.

Jonah grabbed Toby's arm and shouted, "Stop it!"

"I feel sick," said Toby as he started to sway back and forth.

"What's the matter?" Jonah said.

"Why's everything getting fuzzy?" Toby began to fall.

As Jonah reached out to grab Toby, his vision blurred, and then faded to black.

3

MEMPHIS, ANCIENT EGYPT

1400 BCE

Jonah heard someone groan. Toby was lying beside him on the floor. His face was pale and blood trickled from a cut on his forehead. Jonah sat up and shook Toby. "Are you okay?"

Toby opened his eyes. "My head hurts." He touched his head and looked at the blood. "Ugh. I'm going to be sick."

"Not on me you won't!"

"What happened?" Toby's voice was shaking.

"I don't know."

"Jonah?"

"What?"

"I'm scared."

"So am I."

"Jonah?"

"What?"

"Where are we?"

Jonah looked at the massive room and smiled a wobbly grin. "I guess we're not in Kansas anymore."

"Thanks, Dorothy." Toby pointed at Jonah. "Look at what you're wearing."

Jonah tugged at a short, pleated linen cloth wrapped around his lower body and tied at the waist. "We're barefoot, too."

"Where are my Nikes?" Toby cried. "Mom just got them for me!" The watch gleamed in Toby's hand.

"Something happened when you wound the watch," said Jonah. "We must have traveled back in time."

"Maybe if I wind it again, we'll get back home."

Jonah shook his head. "Or maybe we'll end up in some prehistoric cave and get eaten by a dinosaur and never get back," he said. "We have to think before we do anything else."

"Here. Take it." Toby thrust the watch at Jonah. "I don't want it."

Jonah could feel the warmth of the watch in his hand. He pressed the catch and looked at the face. "Something's wrong."

"It's ticking."

"I can hear," said Jonah. "But look. The hour hand is at the six now."

"But it wasn't even five o'clock when I was in your room!"

"I know. But maybe this watch doesn't work like other watches."

"Duh."

Jonah looped the gold chain around his neck and fastened it tightly. Questions swirled inside his head like the rushing waters of a river.

"Jonah, look!" said Toby. "Someone's coming."

The two boys hid behind a pillar as they watched a man approach the altar.

He kneeled in front of a statue with a bird's head. "O Thoth, god of wisdom, help your humble servant, Medjeh, accomplish the great task ahead."

The man called Medjeh held a pottery jug in one hand and two dead ducks in the other. He placed the offerings on a ledge in a small alcove carved into the wall. Then he kneeled down again.

"O let my shadow stick be a true counter of the hours and be pleasing in your sight."

"This is weird," whispered Toby.

"Which part?"

"How come we can understand what that man is saying?"

"It must be part of the magic," Jonah said. "Not only does it make us travel through time, but it's a Universal Translator."

Toby grinned. "That's handy."

Jonah put his finger to his lips and gestured towards Medjeh.

Medjeh stood up and walked over to a table. He picked up a long reed and stuck it in the coals glowing in a charcoal burner in the corner. He lit a stick of incense, placed it in a holder, and spoke aloud as he walked backwards, away from the altar. "Oh gods, let this aroma be pleasing in your sight. Purify this humble man to do your work."

Medjeh turned and called out. "You. Boys."

"Us?" asked Toby.

Medjeh frowned. "Come with me. It is time to go."

"Let's go along with the man for now," whispered Jonah.

"Right," said Toby. "Did you notice that he didn't see the watch?"

"I know," said Jonah. "It's probably because it doesn't belong here."

"Yeah. Neither do we."

They walked through a courtyard lined with pillars on both sides. As they were about to exit through the gate, a bald man wearing a white linen robe and a leopard skin on his shoulder blocked their path.

"Carpenter, a word," the man said.

"Tiras?" Medjeh's voice trembled. "What does the esteemed priest want with me?"

"You promised to deliver the shadow stick many days ago," Tiras hissed. "I still do not see it."

"These things cannot be hurried. One must wait until fortune appoints the day."

Tiras jabbed his finger against Medjeh's chest. "When I am ready, the gods are ready." He pressed his lips together. "Do I make myself clear?"

Medjeh swallowed hard. "Yes. Perfectly."

"Tomorrow I shall have it," said Tiras, "or you will suffer the consequences." He turned and walked into the temple.

Medjeh took a deep breath. "Come, boys. We must leave." The setting sun beat down on his bare back and gleamed on his oiled hair as he walked ahead of them.

At that moment, a man bumped into Jonah. He wore a sweatshirt, khaki pants, and an old pair of sneakers. His hair was white and bushy. His brow was furrowed; his eyes were deep-set and worried. The man opened his mouth to say something but just then, Toby pushed Jonah and called out, "Come on! I'll race you!"

When Jonah looked back, the man had vanished. *This is crazy,* he thought. *Now people are starting to appear and disappear into thin air.*

Medjeh began to speak when the boys caught up to him. "Your father sent you here to Memphis, to this city of craftsmen," he said. "You must learn your trade well and make him proud."

"Did you hear that?" whispered Toby. "He said 'Memphis.'" Toby pretended to play the guitar. He began to sing "You Ain't Nothin' but a Hound Dog".

"Cut it out," snapped Jonah. "You're not Elvis and this isn't a joke."

Toby's smile vanished. "I know."

Medjeh droned on. "You will learn to be master carpenters and thus bring honour to your family." He wagged his finger. "As the wise men say: 'Take counsel with all, for it is possible to learn from all.'"

"What's he talking about?" whispered Toby.

"I don't know," Jonah murmured.

"I want to go home." Toby's eyes filled with tears.

"Me too."

Medjeh stopped in front of a house made of mud bricks and coated with limestone plaster. Grille windows were set high up on the walls.

"Here we are," Medjeh said. "Home at last."

They entered the house, passed through a workshop, and walked into the living room where a substantial wood column held up the roof.

"Look, Jonah!" Toby pointed to coloured flowers and designs painted on the walls. "I'd love to paint those."

A pale silver cat with charcoal spots all over its body was curled up on a low stool. It yawned lazily as they passed. The boys followed Medjeh to a stairway at one end of the room. The cat roused itself from the stool and padded along behind them.

A servant woman followed, bringing linen cloths and a bowl of warm water that smelled of flowers. Before going up the stairs, Medjeh and the boys washed their hands.

"Here. Let me wash that cut," said Jonah. "We've got to get rid of the germs."

"Thanks."

"Dad will kill me if anything happens to you."

"He will? But he doesn't care about me," said Toby. "He talks about you all the time."

"He does —?"

"What is this word 'germs'?" Medjeh asked as he dried his hands.

"Nothing," Jonah mumbled. "A word from our town." *I have to be more careful. Things from the future aren't supposed to be brought into the past. I learned that from reruns of* Star Trek.

"I see." Medjeh turned to the servant. "Bring food and drink up to the roof. We will eat there tonight. Perhaps we will catch a cool breeze from the north. Tell your mistress I am home."

"Yes, master."

Medjeh and the boys climbed up the stairs to the flat roof. They sat down on a reed mat under a canopy supported by six poles. The cat jumped into Jonah's lap and started to purr.

The servant appeared on the roof and placed a pitcher of beer and four cups on a low wooden table next to where Medjeh and the boys were sitting. Medjeh poured beer for himself and the boys. He gulped noisily.

"The gods have been kind to us," he said. "We have so many trees ..." He had a faraway look in his eyes. "My favourites are from foreign lands: cedar, cypress, and juniper from Lebanon and Syria; ebony from Africa."

"What's this, Medjeh? Are you going on and on about your trees again?" a woman said as she climbed the last few steps to the rooftop.

Medjeh shook himself. "Ah, Nefret!" He stood up and walked towards his wife. The strong aroma of her perfume wafted over to Jonah.

Nefret wore an ankle-length, sleeveless linen dress. Her eyes were rimmed with green and her lips were stained red. Her short black hair was combed and oiled. She looked at the boys coldly. With an impatient gesture, she waved them away.

The cat jumped up and ran to a corner where it started to lick its paws. The boys moved to another mat nearby. Jonah listened intently to their conversation while Toby picked up a piece of charcoal and began to draw on a scrap of wood he had found.

"Sit down, dear wife, sit down."

The servant reappeared with a platter of flat bread, grilled fish, and lentils that smelled of garlic and onions. She placed the food on the table and backed away.

"I went to the temple today," Medjeh said. "I made a special sacrifice to the gods."

"Why?" Nefret scooped up fish and lentils with a piece of bread.

"To ask for their aid," Medjeh said. "To make the shadow stick." Nefret patted her hair. "Nefret, are you listening to me?"

"Of course, dear husband," Nefret answered as she chewed her food.

"I'm hungry," whispered Toby.

"So am I," said Jonah.

Toby elbowed Jonah. "Let's ask for something to eat."

"I have a feeling we're not supposed to."

Medjeh picked up a piece of bread and wrapped it around some fish. The boys stared at him intently. So did the cat.

"Here, boys," said Medjeh. He piled some food on a small platter and beckoned to Jonah to take it. He put a piece of fish on the ground for the cat, which sniffed it suspiciously before grabbing it with his sharp teeth.

Toby broke off a piece of bread and began to chew. But then he spit it out. "Ugh," he whispered. "This tastes like sand!"

"We'd better eat something," said Jonah. "Who knows when we'll eat again?"

"I don't care. It's hard and gritty."

"Toby, chew," ordered Jonah.

"All right already!" Toby chewed the bread. "A little beer should wash it down." He grinned as he reached for his cup.

"You're too young to drink beer!" said Jonah.

"And you're not?"

"I guess you've got a point there."

Medjeh was speaking. "The astrologer said that tomorrow will be a lucky day."

"It's about time!" Nefret said. "I wondered when you were finally going to make that tiresome sun stick, or whatever it is called." She looked worried. "Tiras has been sending angry messages. He grows impatient."

Jonah strained to hear what Medjeh said. "If the shadow stick is not ready, Tiras warned me … I will be punished … sent for hard labour to the quarries."

"No!" Nefret gasped.

"Who knows what Tiras will do? He will not accept more delays." Medjeh shuddered. "He will come down on my head like a sandstorm from the desert."

"Do not worry, husband," Nefret said. "Tomorrow will be a lucky day."

"I hope so." Medjeh looked up at the darkening sky. A star or two cast its faint light. He sighed. "Ah well, night follows day, and day follows night. The sky goddess Nut has swallowed Ra, the setting sun. Tomorrow she will give birth to him again."

Medjeh glanced at the boys. "It is late, young ones. Go downstairs to the small bedroom. We must rise early in the morning."

"Come on, Toby," said Jonah.

"I'm coming." Toby tried to stand up but started to sway back and forth.

"What's the matter with you?"

Toby grinned. "I guess I drank too much of that beer."

"We don't have far to go," Jonah said. He put an arm around Toby's shoulders. "Lean on me."

"Hey, Jonah," Toby said.

"What?"

"Want to hear a song I just made up?"

"No," Jonah snapped.

Toby ignored him and began to sing.

> It's great to have a brother
> To go through time together,
> No matter what the weather,
> We'll always stick together.

"*So* corny!" Jonah said.

"Admit it's good."

Jonah rolled his eyes. "Okay. It's good."

They walked downstairs, the cat following them with dainty steps.

Toby lay down on a mat of woven reeds. Beside them, the cat licked himself from his pointed ears to his striped tail. Then he curled up in a ball at Jonah's feet and began to purr softly.

Jonah couldn't shake his guilt and worry. *Why did I steal the watch? And how will we ever get back home?* Hours passed before he finally fell asleep.

"Wake up, boys!" Medjeh's finger was poking Jonah's shoulder. The cat yawned, showing his pink gums and sharp teeth. His breath smelled of fish.

"But ... it's still dark," said Toby.

"Hurry!" said Medjeh. "We must finish our task before the rays of the sun reach the top of the sky."

The boys joined Medjeh in the kitchen where they ate a hasty meal of bread and dates.

"Still sandy," Toby muttered.

"Shut up and eat," Jonah said.

When they were finished, they followed Medjeh into the workshop. He picked up two pieces of wood. One piece was rectangular; the other was shaped like a fat "T".

"Boys, bring my tools," Medjeh ordered. "Awl, drill, saw, and mallet."

"What are those?" whispered Jonah.

"I'll show you," said Toby.

"How do you know that stuff?"

"I read about them in a book about sculpture," Toby said.

"Smart aleck," said Jonah as he poked his elbow into Toby's ribs.

"Ow!"

They put the tools into a large basket and followed the carpenter outside. Medjeh kneeled down and bowed his head in front of a small statue. "Ptah, god of craftsmen, give me the skill needed for this task." Medjeh paused, opened his eyes, and stood up. "It is time."

He picked up the awl and mallet, took a deep breath, and with one sharp stroke made a hole near the end of the rectangular piece of wood.

"Young one," Medjeh said to Jonah. "Take this piece and drill a hole here." He added, "The length of ... your pointing finger."

Jonah sat down on a low stool and started to pull the bow drill back and forth. With each pull, the metal dug deeper into the wood.

Meanwhile, Medjeh started another hole with the awl, this time on top of the T-shaped piece of wood. His face dripped with sweat as he drilled into the hard wood.

"You," he called to Toby. "Finish this hole."

The sun was almost overhead when they had completed their tasks.

"Give me your piece," said Medjeh. He looked at Jonah's work and nodded in satisfaction. "Good. That will do." Placing the "T" piece on top of the rectangular piece, the carpenter said, "Now, hold them tightly together."

Jonah held one piece while Toby held the other. Medjeh hammered a long, wooden peg through both holes. Only when he had finished did he pause to wipe the sweat from his face and neck.

Medjeh shaded his eyes and looked up at the sun. "Almost time." He carefully placed the long part of the wood facing towards the east.

"Now, you know the sun travels from its high point and moves towards the west — the land of the dead." Medjeh shuddered. "You must help me mark the divisions on the stick." He handed Jonah a piece of charcoal. "Use this."

"But how will we make the marks?" asked Jonah.

"Ah, that is one of the secrets of the shadow stick," whispered Medjeh. "I will show you —"

"Medjeh! They are here!" Nefret was standing in the doorway. Her dress was wrinkled and her hair was disheveled.

"Who is here?"

"Tiras! And a soldier!"

"O Thoth, save us!" Medjeh looked at the boys. "I must go. With the gods' help, I will return soon."

"Come!" Nefret said.

Rising, Medjeh followed her.

Jonah heard loud voices from inside the house. Medjeh was pleading; Nefret was crying; a man was shouting. Jonah stared at the shadow stick, bent down, and clutched it tightly in his arms.

"What are you doing? Wind the watch," said Toby. "We've got to get away!"

"But who knows where we'll end up?"

"Any place is better than here!"

"I'm not so sure."

"Please, Jonah!"

Tiras, the priest, stood in the doorway. Behind him, a soldier waited at attention.

"Boy, what do you have there?" Tiras nodded. "Ah, the shadow stick." He stretched out his hand. "Give it to me."

"But it's not finished yet!" Jonah said.

"Now, boy," Tiras commanded.

"No! I won't!"

"Jonah, give it to him!" cried Toby.

"Soldier! Take it!" Tiras ordered.

The soldier grabbed Jonah's arms and pulled them behind his back. Jonah struggled, but the soldier was too strong. He yanked the shadow stick away and handed it to Tiras.

"No!" cried Jonah.

"Argue with the priest, will you?" snarled the soldier. He punched Jonah on the back of his head while he held Jonah's arms with his other hand. Then he struck him again.

"Leave him alone!" yelled Toby. He ran towards the soldier and kicked him in the shin. The soldier swatted Toby as if he were a fly. Toby groaned and fell down hard on the ground.

"Toby!" Jonah cried. He turned his head and bit down hard on the soldier's arm. The soldier cried out and let go of Jonah's arms. Jonah's head was pounding. He grabbed the watch, turned the knob, and fell right on top of Toby.

He heard the ticking of the watch. The carpenter's workshop faded into blackness.

4

KAIFENG, CHINA

1094

Toby was shaking Jonah's shoulder. "Are you okay?"

"I've got a splitting headache," said Jonah. "You don't happen to have a Tylenol, do you?"

"I didn't exactly have time to pack."

"Neither did I." Jonah smiled. "But hey, we're here, wherever 'here' is. Maybe it'll be fun."

"But where *are* we?"

"It looks like some kind of market."

"But bigger than any market I've ever seen!"

Throngs of people milled about. Boxes and baskets of fruits and vegetables were piled in front of a jumble of stalls closely packed next to each other. Silk cloth in red, green, and black fluttered on bamboo racks. Sets of blue and white porcelain dishes were displayed on shelves. Pigs squealed, mules brayed, and chickens clucked. The air was filled with the smells of incense, spices, animals, and people.

"Look, Jonah. Your clothes are different again," said Toby.

Jonah was wearing baggy pants and a loose-fitting jacket. "These clothes itch. I bet they're made of hemp."

"Hemp?"

"My mom likes to buy organic food. Lately, she's been buying organic clothes, too."

"Good. When you don't want to wear them anymore, you can eat them."

"Shut up, Toby!"

Toby laughed. "You've got a bun on top of your head. Just like a girl!"

"So do you!"

Toby touched his hair. He stopped laughing. "Great. Just great." He pointed to the watch. "What time does it say?"

"Seven o'clock. But I don't get it. More time passed than an hour!"

Toby looked down at his feet. "I hate this."

"What?"

"Look at my shoes!" Toby wore a pair of sandals made of rope.

"It's better than bare feet."

"Not much."

Jonah noticed a man sitting in front of a group of people. He wore pants and a loose jacket. He had a thin black moustache and a pointed beard. His face was lined around his eyes and mouth. His hair was gathered in a topknot.

"I want to hear what that man is saying," Jonah said. He stood up and Toby followed him as they made their way towards the storyteller.

The man spoke in a singsong voice.

> I have seen a road
> that wanders in green shade,
> That runs through
> sweet fields of flowers.
> My eyes have travelled there,
> and journeyed far
> along that cool fine road.

"A fine poem, Li Po," said a man in the audience. "You are an excellent storyteller."

"How come we understand what he said?" Toby whispered.

"It must be the magic again," said Jonah.

One of the men in the audience called, "Li Po, tell us another story." As the storyteller began to speak and Jonah looked about him.

A man was sitting on the edge of the crowd. He wore a sweatshirt and khaki pants. A ballpoint pen was hooked on the neck of his sweatshirt. His hair was white and bushy — like the top of a dandelion pod.

What's that man doing here? Is he following us? And if so, why? And how? Jonah felt a shiver run up and down his spine. *Toby and I don't belong in this time and place. But neither does this man, this Stranger.*

Jonah took a big breath and was about to walk over to the man when a woman cried out, "Stop! Thief!"

A man yelled, "There! He went that way!"

The thief crashed into a stall. The bamboo poles collapsed, the flimsy roof fell down, and pots and pans rolled and clattered from one end of the market to the other. Dogs barked, chickens squawked, and horses snorted. People ran everywhere, trying to catch the thief.

As the noise subsided, Li Po gestured to the boys. "You boys!" he said. "Come here!"

Jonah looked for the Stranger but he had disappeared.

"Who?" said Jonah.

"Us?" said Toby.

"Yes, you," Li Po said. "I will buy you a bowl of soup now if you promise to help me later."

"Let's go along with him until we figure out what's happening," whispered Jonah.

"Okay," said Toby. "Anyway, I'm starving."

"You're always starving."

Toby grinned. "Well, a person gets hungry travelling through time."

"Do you agree?" said Li Po.

"Yes, sir," said both boys together.

"Come along," said Li Po. "Let us go to Chang's stall. He makes the best soup in Kaifeng."

Jonah's stomach was rumbling like a small earthquake as they walked over to the stall. After taking the bowls, they sat down on a bamboo mat nearby.

While they were eating, a stout man approached them and bowed towards Li Po. "Honourable teller of stories, may I join you?"

"Of course, friend Chang," said Li Po. "Please sit down." The boys moved over.

The man lowered himself to sit beside the story-teller. "It is good to rest after much labour."

"The soup is delicious today," said Li Po. "Boys, this is my friend, Chang."

The boys bowed to the older man.

The soldiers had caught the thief and were pushing him through the market in front of where they were sitting.

Li Po shook his head. "Poor man," he said. "He must have been truly desperate. He will suffer far more from the whipping he gets than from the hunger in his belly."

Jonah choked on the soup and began to cough. *I'm a thief, too*, he thought.

Toby patted him on the back. "Are you okay?"

"Leave me alone," Jonah snapped.

"I was just asking." Toby pulled his hand away, turned his back to Jonah, and picked up a stick. He began to draw a picture of the market on the hard-packed ground.

Chang sighed. "As you know, my friend, Kaifeng is not an easy place to live."

Li Po's bushy eyebrows drew closer together. "Flood and devastation come to us as surely as the Yellow River flows."

"No wonder the river is called 'China's Sorrow,'" Chang said. "But at least today there is good news."

"We must be in China," whispered Toby.

"That's the *where*. But *when*?" Jonah said. *I like Toby*, he thought with surprise. *He doesn't hold a grudge.*

Li Po looked at the boys and put a finger to his lips. "Go on, my friend."

"In this great capital city of the Emperor," Chang said. "This city that holds more than one million people, the Imperial tutor, Su Sung, has completed a structure that has never been built before."

"The astronomical clock?" asked Li Po.

"Hey Toby!" whispered Jonah. "He's talking about clocks!"

"All you think about is clocks!" Toby looked at Jonah's bowl. "Can I have your soup?"

Jonah handed his bowl to Toby. "Here. I never did like bean curd."

Toby made a face. "Bean turd?"

"Bean curd!" Jonah grinned. "It tastes better if you call it tofu." The boys started laughing but Li Po's stern gaze quieted them down.

"To be sure," continued Chang. "They say it is as tall as six men standing one on top of the other...."

"Amazing!" Li Po said.

"Can we go see the clock?" asked Jonah.

"Me too?" echoed Toby. "I want to draw it."

"You must not interrupt your elders!" Li Po scolded. "In the olden days, a boy would be put to death for such rudeness."

Jonah felt his face getting red. "I'm sorry."

"Sorry," echoed Toby.

Li Po turned his attention back to his friend.

"I will tell you something else." Chang lowered his voice. "Only Su Sung and his associates know how the clock works."

"They will never tell," said Li Po, shaking his head.

Chang gestured with one hand slicing across his throat. "Behind the walls of the imperial palace, the Son of Heaven keeps many secrets," he whispered.

"Come," said Li Po. "We must get back to work." He handed the bowls to Chang. The men stood up and bowed to each other.

On their way back, Li Po explained what the boys were supposed to do. "When I have finished telling a story, you must collect money from the people. Can you do that?"

Jonah nodded.

"I hope you will get some paper money as well as coins," sighed Li Po. He sat down again in his corner of the market. A crowd gathered in front of him.

Li Po told a story about a brave young man who set out on a long journey to retrieve the family treasure that thieves had stolen. After many adventures, he accomplished his goal and brought honour to his family.

"I wish we could find treasure," whispered Toby.

"We don't need treasure. We just need to get home."

Toby nodded. "Yeah, but how?"

Jonah shook his head. "I wish I knew. Come on. The story's finished."

The boys stood up and walked through the crowd. People tossed money on their bamboo trays.

As the day passed, Li Po told more stories and the boys collected more copper coins.

The sky began to turn pink and mauve. Wisps of cloud floated high above the market. The smells of grilled meat and vegetables filled the air.

"It was a good day," said Li Po. He looked intently at the boys. "Tell me, do you have a place to sleep tonight?"

Jonah shook his head. "No, we've just arrived."

"You can say that again!" whispered Toby.

"Then you will come home with me."

"Thank you," said Jonah and Toby together.

"And may we see the astronomical clock tomorrow?" asked Jonah.

"I too would like to see this wonderful invention." Li Po nodded. "Yes, we will go tomorrow."

Jonah clapped his hands. "Thank you!"

Li Po smiled. "You are a good boy."

Jonah felt his face growing red. *I don't deserve any praise*, he thought. *I'm a thief. Worse still, I stole from my own father. I'm glad Li Po can't read my mind.*

"Tonight I will play cards with my friends," said Li Po, "and tomorrow we will see the wonderful clock Su Sung has made."

The next morning dawned clear and mild. Sparrows were chirping in the trees and a fresh breeze blew in from the mountains.

Long before they came to the site of the astronomical clock, Jonah heard the creaking of gears and the splashing of water. "Stay near me," warned Li Po. "There are many people here. Do not get lost."

They came to a tower that rose high above their heads. Guards wearing light armour and swords on their belts stood at regular intervals around the tower.

A guide was talking to a group of people clustered around him. "This edifice was built over two years ago.

"The tower is more than thirty feet high. It is surmounted by an enormous armillary sphere made of bronze. A celestial globe inside the tower rotates automatically. One can observe the heavenly bodies from the observation platform above."

"Wouldn't it be great to be at the top?" Toby whispered. "To see everything from there, and draw a picture of the whole scene?"

"Only if you want to get into trouble," said Jonah.

"As you can see," said the guide, pointing upwards, "the front of the tower is five storeys tall. Each storey has a door through which carved figures appear on the hour.

"The figures ring bells and gongs. They hold tablets to indicate the hours and other special times of the day and night. Inside the tower is the source of all the power — a great scoop-wheel that uses water and turns the shafts that operate the various devices." The guide waved. "Now we will go to the other side."

"Come along," urged Li Po, as he followed the guide.

I should follow Li Po, Jonah thought. *But I wish I could see the water wheel and then climb the stairs right to the top.*

"The wheel is checked by an 'escapement' consisting of a sort of weigh-bridge which prevents the fall of a scoop until full and ..." The voice of the guide faded away as the group followed him to the other side of the tower.

A movement caught Jonah's eye. Someone was climbing the stairs. It was Toby! He'd gone up after all — probably to draw a picture! *I have to get him down before anyone else sees him!*

Jonah ran towards the tower and began to climb the steps.

"Boy! Stop!" a guard shouted.

Jonah ignored him. There was no time to explain. He turned a ninety-degree corner and climbed more steps.

The guard started up after Jonah. His armour and heavy steps sounded loudly in Jonah's ears. The man caught up to Jonah and grabbed the back of his jacket. "You must not go up!" he puffed. "It is forbidden!"

Jonah hung onto the handrail and tried to pull himself free. Finally, he gave one tremendous kick and the guard went tumbling down the stairs.

"Toby! Wait!" cried Jonah.

Toby looked over his shoulder. "Jonah?"

"Come down," Jonah gasped. Just a few more steps. He could almost touch Toby now.

"You! Boys! Stop!" Two guards were climbing the stairs. Their short swords were raised.

"We've got to get out of here!" cried Toby. He reached for Jonah's arm.

"Hang on!" Jonah wound the watch. Far below, he could see Li Po waving his arms and shouting at them. Everything spun around — the noisy market, the winding Yellow River, the people far below.

A gong tolled the hours.

5

THE MONASTERY OF LE THORONET, FRANCE

1205

"Bestir yourself, boy!" a man said. "I need more light here."

Jonah opened his eyes. The embers of a fire glowed faintly in the hearth. He felt the heavy weight of the watch hanging from his neck. *I've landed in another place, in another time.*

Jonah looked around. *Where's Toby? Did I leave him back in China, or has he jumped forward somewhere different? Toby's a pain sometimes, but I'm older; I should take care of him. Oh, how I wish I'd never seen the watch!*

"Do you hear me, boy?" Jonah's thoughts disappeared like wisps of smoke. He stood up and brushed the dust from the grey tunic he was wearing.

The man sat at a wooden desk. Behind him, several tall bookcases leaned against stone walls. Old books and leather-bound manuscripts filled the shelves.

Candlelight shone on the man's face. As Jonah came closer, the man looked up from the parchment he was writing on. "Is something bothering you, boy?" he asked in a gentle voice.

Jonah shook his head. *How can I explain I've been transported back in time? I can hardly believe it myself.*

The man was speaking. "I, Brother Albert, am only a humble monk who tries to do God's work in this monastery." He smiled. "Daylight is fading and the candle is almost spent." He squinted at Jonah with warm brown eyes. "Even God's work needs light. Go to the kitchen and fetch another candle, if you please. And hurry back as quickly as you can!"

Brother Albert sent Jonah away with a wave of his hand. "Now, let me see. Where was I?" he mumbled as he began to sharpen his quill with a knife.

Jonah didn't dare disturb Brother Albert to ask for directions. He hurried out of the library, ran along a passageway, turned the corner to another corridor, and bumped right into the biggest man he had ever seen in his life.

"Now look what you've made me do!" cried the monk. Loaves of bread tumbled onto the floor while a large wheel of cheese rolled over to the wall. The monk stooped down to pick up the bread. *He looks like a mother hen trying to gather her chicks together,* Jonah thought. He almost laughed but he didn't dare.

"As if I don't have enough work to do — feeding over fifty men and boys," the monk grumbled. He glared at Jonah. "Don't just stand there! Pick up that cheese over there!"

"Sorry," said Jonah. "I was trying to find the kitchen."

Anne Dublin

"Say 'Sorry Brother Pierre,'" the man demanded.

"Sorry, Brother Pierre."

Brother Pierre dusted off the bread with a corner of his robe. "Are you a new member of our community? I do not remember seeing you here before."

Jonah swallowed hard. "My name is Jonah."

"A good name from the Bible." Brother Pierre frowned. "But it does not excuse your clumsiness."

Jonah handed the cheese to Brother Pierre and followed him along the corridor. "Come along now," said Brother Pierre. "Here is the kitchen."

Jonah backed away, leaving room for Brother Pierre's huge body to slip in sideways through the doorway. Jonah took a deep breath and followed Brother Pierre.

"What are you looking for?" asked Brother Pierre.

"Candles for Brother Albert."

Brother Pierre pointed to a high shelf. "Take them and be gone, before you make me drop something else!"

Jonah grabbed two beeswax candles and after a few wrong turns, found his way back to the library.

"There you are!" Brother Albert looked up from his work. "I had almost given up on you." He chuckled. "I thought I would have to write in the dark!"

"Here's one candle," panted Jonah, "and I brought another one for later."

"Well, you're a big help, as God is my witness." Brother Albert shivered. "What did you say your name was?"

"Jonah."

"Well then, Jonah, I know I should not think of my comfort, but these old bones are aching with the cold. Kindly put more wood on the fire." He winked. "And we won't tell Brother Pierre about it, will we?"

"Yes, Brother Albert. I mean, no, Brother Albert." Jonah placed a dry log on the fire.

Brother Albert handed Jonah a mortar and pestle. "Help me now. Take this stick of ink and grind it into a fine powder."

Jonah sat down on a low stool by the fire, put the ink in the mortar, and started to grind it with the pestle. The only sounds were the scratching of goose quill on parchment, pestle on mortar, and the winter wind rattling the windowpanes. Jonah's face grew warm; his back stayed cold.

"Brother Albert?" asked Jonah.

"Hmm?"

"What are you writing?"

Brother Albert looked up. He beckoned to Jonah. "Come closer. I will show you."

Jonah stood up and walked over to the desk.

"I am copying the writings of Augustine." A yellowed parchment lay open on the desk, but Jonah could not make out the faded letters.

"How old is it?" asked Jonah.

"What? Oh, hundreds of years."

"But where did it come from?"

"A childhood friend of mine, a knight returning from the Crusades, found it in an old library near Rome. He knows I am interested in these writings.

Besides, he gave it to the monastery as a penance for some wrongdoing." Brother Albert peered at Jonah in the dim light. "It is very valuable," he said. "It is a rare manuscript beyond price."

A loud bell rang out to disturb the silence.

"*Laudate deum*," said the monk. "It is time for *Vespers* and then our meal. You are new here, are you not?"

"Yes," stammered Jonah.

"Then I will explain. We pray eight times during a twenty-four hour period — seven times during the day and one time at night."

I wish I could whistle, Jonah thought. *But I have a feeling that Brother Albert wouldn't like it.*

"We sleep for six hours, work for six, read for four, and attend prayers for eight." Brother Albert wiped his quill, covered the inkpot, and rose from his bench. "Come now. All things at their proper time. We must not be late."

A wooden altar stood in front of a plain stone wall at the east end of the church. A simple wooden cross hung above the altar. Candles on the altar cast flickering shadows on the walls and on the faces and robes of the monks.

Brother Albert sat with the monks on one side of the rectangular room. Jonah joined the lay brothers and servants on the other side. The abbot took his place in front to lead the monks in prayer.

The chanting voices rose and fell. They filled the chapel and echoed off the walls. Jonah sat on the hard bench and looked around. Toby was grinning and waving at him from where he sat on the end of the bench.

Jonah felt his body relax, as if a great weight had been lifted from him. He moved over to sit beside Toby.

"Where were you?" Jonah whispered.

"I was in the kitchen. This enormous monk made me scrub out a million pots and pans." Toby held out his red hands. "I've got dishpan hands." He smiled wanly. "And still no Nikes," he said, looking down at his leather sandals.

"I was worried about you!"

"You were?" said Toby. "But you don't even like me!"

"Well, you're getting to grow on me." Jonah made a face. "Like a fungus."

Toby moved closer to Jonah. "Do you know where we are?"

"At a monastery. Somewhere in France."

"And I guess we understand French?"

"Luckily," said Jonah. "My worst subject in school."

"Jonah?"

"What?"

"I'm hungry."

"What else is new?" Jonah smiled.

"Shh!" hissed a monk sitting across from them. The man's face had even features that might have made him look handsome, but it was marred by a sour expression.

"Who's that?" said Toby.

"That is Brother Bernard," whispered a boy beside them. "Yesterday, I returned with him from the monastery at Sénanque." The boy sighed. "My name is Paul."

Prayers were over. The boys followed Paul to the dining room. Bread and cheese were set out on long wooden tables. Two brothers ladled out savoury bowls of soup.

After grace, Toby tore off a piece of bread and began to chew. "Why does the bread taste so dusty?"

Jonah smiled. "I don't know. But at least it doesn't have sand in it, like in Egypt!"

"Yeah. Anything's better than that!"

"Where are you from?" asked Paul.

There was an uncomfortable silence. "Uh ... from up north," Jonah said.

"Yeah. There," said Toby.

"You two are not much for conversation, are you?" said Paul.

"Not much to say," said Jonah. *If Paul only knew.*

Paul shrugged. "We had better get some rest. *Laudes* will be in a few hours."

After they had finished eating, the boys walked to the dormitory. Jonah lay down on a straw pallet on the floor and pulled a rough woollen blanket up to his chin. He felt utterly exhausted. He was drifting off to sleep when Toby shook him.

"Jonah?"

"What?"

"How are we going to get home?"

"I don't know." Jonah touched the watch around his neck. "All I know is that this watch has some kind of magic in it. I think we're supposed to go where it takes us."

"I guess so." Toby swallowed hard. "Jonah?"

"What?"

"I miss my mom."

"I miss mine, too." Jonah patted Toby on the back. "Let's get some sleep."

After breakfast the next morning, Jonah felt a heavy hand on his shoulder. "There you are, young fellow!" Jonah looked up and saw a stout, red-faced monk standing behind him. "I need your help."

"But I have to go to the library," Jonah said. "Brother Albert asked me to see him this morning."

"You need to help me, Brother Gabriel, first." Jonah had the feeling that when Brother Gabriel asked you to do something, you did it.

"Toby, will you tell Brother Albert I'll be late?"

"Sure. Maybe he'll let me borrow a pen and ink to draw a picture."

Jonah followed Brother Gabriel out of the dining room and along a corridor. They soon came to a work-room on one side of the cloister.

Brother Gabriel pointed to a large iron bowl with lines etched on the inside. "I need your help with this water clock."

"The clepsydra?" Jonah asked. "That's so cool!"

"'Cool?' What do you mean?"

"Nothing," Jonah mumbled.

Brother Gabriel shrugged. "It is my job to keep track of the hours for prayer. I am in charge of the water clock, the sundial, and the sandglasses."

"I love clocks," said Jonah wistfully.

"As do I," said Brother Gabriel, smiling for the first time. "The abbot says, 'Time belongs to the community and to God.'"

He patted the clepsydra. "She's been having trouble keeping good time. It is too cold for her, like for us." He shook his head at the water clock as if it were a beloved child he was disappointed in. "The water keeps freezing in her.

"Now this is what you must do: Empty out all the water. Then scrub her out real good with this brush — all round the sides, inside and out. And don't forget to check the hole at the bottom and clean it out, too. I'll be back before midday prayers, to check for leaks and fill her up again with fresh water."

"But how will you tell the hours meanwhile?"

"Not to worry." Brother Gabriel patted a small instrument hanging from the rope around his ample waist. "See this? It is a portable sundial with a folding pointer." He gestured towards the water clock. "Now get to work. There's something else I need to do."

Jonah's stomach was rumbling. It had been several hours since the morning meal. He finished scrubbing the clepsydra and walked towards the window. If he stood on tiptoe, he could see a corner of the garden. He inhaled deeply. The air was still cold but the bright sunlight gave the illusion of warmth.

At the furthest end of the garden, someone was standing under an oak tree. The smoke from his pipe rose up into the clear air. He took the pipe out of his mouth and looked intently at Jonah. He wore khaki pants and a sweatshirt, and sneakers on his feet. *He's the same man,* Jonah thought. *He's the Stranger who was in Egypt and in China. How did he get here, too? Why is he following us? What does he want?*

Jonah touched the watch hanging from his neck. *Does the watch have something to do with the Stranger?* he wondered. *Does it belong to him? Can the Stranger help us get home?*

Jonah took a big breath and decided to go to the garden. He would confront the Stranger and get answers to his questions. But then he froze. Someone else was in the garden. The Stranger put his finger to his lips as if to warn Jonah to be quiet.

A monk with his back to Jonah was kneeling on the ground. He looked nervously about him as he hacked away at the earth with a small shovel. He placed something in the hole he had dug and quickly covered it with earth.

When he stood up and turned around, Jonah saw it was Brother Bernard. He stood up and brushed the dirt from his robe. His expression was as sour as ever.

Jonah moved back behind the window frame. He didn't know why, but he didn't want Brother Bernard to see him.

Just then, Brother Gabriel rushed into the room. "Boy!" The monk's voice was trembling. "Come quick!"

"What's the matter?"

"We must ring the bell!"

"But why?"

"Quickly!" He beckoned Jonah to follow him. Jonah glanced back into the garden. There was no sign of the Stranger or Brother Bernard. Jonah and Brother Gabriel rushed to the back of the church and climbed up a narrow set of stairs to the bell tower.

Over and over, they pulled and released the thick rope attached to a large bell high above them. The sound of the bell rang within the monastery and outside its walls to the countryside beyond.

"Everyone must have heard the ringing by now," Jonah said.

"I hope so," said Brother Gabriel. "We must go now."

In the chapter house, men and boys sat uneasily on wooden benches placed around the walls. They spoke in hushed voices.

Jonah sat down beside Toby. "What happened?"

Toby shook his head and pointed to the abbot.

"My brothers," the abbot said. "I have grievous news." His face was ashen; the lines on his forehead and around his mouth seemed to have grown deeper since the previous day.

"Early this morning, our dear Brother Albert was found in the library. He was stabbed with a knife." The brothers gasped. Jonah felt as if a fist were clutching his heart.

The abbot continued. "He lies gravely wounded." He bowed his head. "Let us pray."

Monks, lay brothers, and servants alike all bowed their heads and prayed in silence. One monk began to sing a song and the others joined in:

> Brief life is here our portion,
> Brief sorrow, short-lived care;
> The life that knows no ending,
> The tearless life is there.
> O happy retribution, short toil,
> eternal rest.
> For mortals and for sinners, a mansion
> with the blessed.

The day faded into night as the monks chanted more prayers for healing. Their hearts were filled with worry for their friend and companion.

Jonah could not sleep that night. Brother Albert's face kept appearing in his head amid swirling images of quills and knives and yellowing manuscripts. Every part of his body felt like a twisted knot.

In the middle of the night, he got up from his straw pallet, put on his tunic and sandals, and walked softly to the cloister. He inhaled the tang of pine trees and listened to the gurgle of the river further down the hill. High above, he heard the screeching call of an owl.

Someone tapped him on his shoulder and Jonah turned around with a start. His heart was pounding. It was Toby.

"What are you doing here?" Jonah whispered.

"I heard you get up. I didn't want to be alone."

"Okay, but be quiet."

Toby nodded. "Who's that?"

Jonah saw two men standing in the shadows on the other side of the cloister. He strained to hear what they were saying while Toby leaned over his shoulder.

"Here it is," whispered the first man. "Just like I promised." He was holding a roll of parchment.

"Here's your money," said the second man. Jonah heard the jingle of coins.

Thou shall not steal, thought Jonah.

"Go quickly. Before someone sees you," said the first man.

The second man placed the parchment inside his cloak. "A pleasure doing business with you," he said. "Until the next time." He pulled his hood over his head and slinked away into the shadows.

The first man turned around. With a gasp, Jonah recognized Brother Bernard. "Come on," he whispered to Toby. "We've got to get out of here!" He took a step back but his foot struck a loose stone in the walkway. The sound echoed loudly against the stone walls.

Brother Bernard raised his head and sniffed the air like a hound after a rabbit.

Jonah held his breath. He could feel Toby trembling beside him. He wanted to run but felt frozen against the wall.

Brother Bernard stalked up to the boys. He grabbed Jonah with one hand and Toby with the other. "What are you two doing here?"

"Nothing," Jonah stammered.

"Nothing?" Brother Bernard shook Jonah until his teeth rattled. "What did you see?"

"Nothing," gasped Jonah.

"We were ... going to bed," said Toby.

Suspicion shone in Brother Bernard's black eyes.

"Let go!" Jonah pleaded. He struggled to get away, but Brother Bernard's fingers dug into his arm.

"Why should I?" Brother Bernard said. "You will tell the abbot and the others what you saw."

"No, I promise," said Jonah.

"We won't," said Toby.

Brother Bernard's fingers felt like iron claws. "I didn't see anything," Jonah said through chattering teeth.

"Do you think I am a fool?" said Brother Bernard. "I do not believe you!"

Brother Bernard half-dragged, half-pushed the boys out of the cloister, through the garden, and down to the river. Jonah stumbled in the dark as Brother Bernard shoved them into the cold mud of the riverbank.

"Sit down," Brother Bernard ordered, "Be quiet, both of you. Or else." He yanked the rope off Jonah's tunic and tied the boys together, back to back. The night was dark with only a thin sliver of moon shining on the black river. Jonah's legs were shaking so hard they hurt. He tried to move, but the rope was too tight.

Brother Bernard seemed to have forgotten about the boys. He began to talk to someone only he could see. "You looked so proud when you left for the Holy Land." He paced back and forth, hitting his fist in the palm of his other hand.

"Toby," Jonah whispered. "Let's try to crawl up the riverbank together."

"Anything to get away from that crazy man!"

Using their elbows and knees, their feet and wrists, they began to squirm away from the sound of the tortured voice.

"You said, 'Little brother, why do you stay behind these cloistered walls when there is a holy war to wage? Come with me and we will fight the infidels together!'" His voice cracked. "But I would not go."

Brother Bernard paused. "Now you are rotting in a Turkish jail, waiting for money to ransom your life...."

Jonah's foot slipped on the wet ground. He started to slide down the slope, dragging Toby along with him. The rough earth scraped his legs, his arms, his face.

Brother Bernard shook his head and stared at the boys. "What are *you* doing here?" His look became hard. "Oh. Now I remember. The little spies!" He grabbed their arms and began to push the boys towards the river. "An accident. No one will ever know."

"No! Let me go!" screamed Jonah as he struggled to get away.

"Help!" cried Toby.

"Be quiet, you maggots!" Brother Bernard growled.

"Please let us go!" begged Jonah.

"Help!" Toby called again.

Jonah kicked the man's leg with all his might, but it was like kicking the trunk of a tree.

Brother Bernard pushed Jonah and Toby down to the ground. "It's all your fault. This wasn't your business."

Jonah struggled but the man was too strong. Brother Bernard took off his belt and tied their feet together. "You wouldn't understand," he panted. "You never wanted something ... so much ... you would risk your eternal soul ... to get it?" He began to push the boys towards the water.

I do understand, Jonah thought desperately. His hands ached; his legs felt numb; his head was throbbing.

All at once, a voice boomed out, "Stop!" Brother Pierre and Brother Gabriel were hurrying towards the river.

"What in God's name are you doing?" Brother Pierre shouted. He grabbed Brother Bernard by the robe and shook him like a wet rag.

"Nothing," said Brother Bernard.

"Nothing?" said Brother Pierre. "What do you mean 'nothing'?"

"He tied us up!" cried Toby.

"He was going to drown us!" said Jonah.

"They were going to tell everyone!" croaked Brother Bernard.

Brother Pierre stood still and asked, "About what?"

Brother Bernard hung his head. He refused to answer.

"Don't move if you know what's good for you," said Brother Pierre.

Brother Gabriel untied Jonah and Toby.

"Come along now," said Brother Pierre. "The abbot shall deal with you."

"No! Please!" cried Brother Bernard. He struggled to break free from Brother Pierre's grasp.

"Come, Brother Bernard," said Brother Gabriel more gently. "Come back up to the monastery." A bell was ringing. "Do you hear the bell? It is time for *Laudes.*"

"'*Laudes?*'" Brother Bernard stood still, as if he did not know where he was.

"Come along now," Brother Pierre coaxed. "And you, boys. Follow us," he called over his shoulder.

Jonah rubbed his sore arms. His body ached with hurt and weariness. "Thanks for being with me, Toby. And Toby?"

"What?"

"I'm sorry I was so mean to you."

"It's okay. That's what brothers do," said Toby.

"I guess."

"Should we leave now?"

"I think so," said Jonah. "Let's hope the next place is better than here."

"I hope it's warmer!" said Toby, shivering.

"It's sure to be another adventure! But Toby?"

"What?"

"Try to stay with me this time!"

Jonah wound the watch. The bell from the monastery was ringing, marking the hour for prayers.

6

PRAGUE, BOHEMIA

1495

Jonah opened his eyes. The steady sound of metal grinding against metal — click, click, click — echoed in the empty room. Cold, musty air seeped into his body.

He was wearing a woolen jacket and linen shirt. A frayed leather belt held up his pants and a cloth hat was on his head.

He stood up and walked over to a small window. He gazed down on the rooftops of a city far below. *Where am I? When am I? And most important, where is Toby?*

He touched the watch. *I hate it,* he thought. *I want to go home. Anything's better than this rushing through time and space. Even if Mom and Dad are divorced, it's better than this.*

The sound of rusty door hinges creaked far below. A door opened and closed. Jonah held his breath. Somebody was coming up the stairs. Tap, step, step. Tap, step, step. The sound stopped.

"Who's there?" a man asked in a quavering voice. "Who's there, I said!" the man repeated, this time louder. Jonah crouched in the shadows. "I know someone's there! I can hear you! Smell you, too!"

The man had reached the top of the stairs and blocked Jonah's way out of the tower room. His pants and jacket were clean but had been patched in several places. He had a trimmed beard and his long grey hair partially concealed unseeing eyes that stared in Jonah's direction. Gnarled hands grasped a walking stick.

Jonah stood up. "Please, sir."

The man stiffened. "Who are you?" He raised his stick, ready to strike.

"My name is Jonah."

"What are you doing here?"

"Please," said Jonah. "Put that down."

"Not till I get some answers! Are you one of those ruffians who like to hide in my tower? Drinking and making trouble?"

"No. I was hiding, but ... just for a few minutes. I'll go now."

"Not so fast," said the man. "Why were you hiding?"

"It's hard to explain. I meant no harm." Jonah swallowed hard. "Truly I didn't."

The man paused. "Your voice is a kind one." He lowered his stick, felt for a stool placed against the wall, and sat down heavily.

"Please, sir. Can you tell me where we are?"

"Why, in Prague of course."

"And ... what year is it?"

"Are you slow, boy? It is the year 1495."

"1495?"

"Yes, of course," said the man. "Much has happened in the world these last few years." He paused. "A New World has been discovered."

"I've heard that." *In 1492, Columbus sailed the ocean blue.* "Columbus is a great explorer."

"You are right." The man squinted in Jonah's direction, as if trying to make out his features. "You have had some schooling?"

Jonah nodded, but then realized the man could not see him. "I should go now." *Maybe I can find Toby somewhere in this city.*

The man hesitated. "You might want to wait a bit."

"Why?"

"The clock is going to strike. Yes. Now!" All at once, there was a loud scraping of metal and a turning of gears. The ringing of a bell sounded against the stone walls and wooden rafters. Jonah held his hands over his ears and tried to muffle the pounding that reverberated in every part of his body. Even after the sound had stopped, his ears kept ringing.

It was silent again, except for the steady clicking of metal against metal. Jonah took his hands away from his ears. His breathing began to slow down. "How did you know?"

"What?"

"That it was going to ring. Right then."

"Who else should know?" The man straightened his back and pointed to himself. "I am Hanus, master clockmaker. I built this clock five years ago — to track time; to use time."

"But ... how could you? You're ..."

Hanus snorted. "Blind? Yes, now I am," he said. "But I was not blind then. Oh, no. Then I was the best clockmaker in Prague — perhaps in all of Europe."

"What happened, sir?" Jonah sat down on the floor near Hanus's feet.

"Damn town council! They hired me to build the clock. Then they became afraid I would build another one, bigger and better, for some other town.

"They paid ruffians to come here while I was working. They tied me up and dragged me to the fire." He shuddered. "The bastards ... put out my eyes ... with a poker!" Hanus spit on the floor. "As if that would stop other people from making a clock like mine!" He pointed to his head. "It is all in here. They cannot take that away from me."

He stood up but his body was bent like a tree that had weathered too many storms.

"Can I ... take you somewhere?" Jonah asked.

"Take me home, boy. It is not far from here."

When they came out of the tower, Jonah looked up at the clock. The rays of the setting sun shone on its face and made it glow like the dying embers of a fire. The church spires glistened and birds twittered in the trees. *This is a beautiful city,* Jonah thought. *But where's Toby?*

Hanus leaned on Jonah's arm. "Just a few blocks this way," he said. "Along Parizska Street, then turn right on Kostecna."

Jonah tried to ignore people's stares as they made their way along the cobblestone streets. *Hanus and*

I must look like a strange pair, he thought. *A ragged boy and an old, blind man.*

"Home at last," Hanus said. "Come inside."

"But …"

"Just for a minute. I want you to meet my daughter." He put his arm around Jonah's shoulders and gently pushed him forward into the house.

A table stood at the centre of the room, with benches on either side. Several stools were scattered about the room and a low cupboard stood on one side. The walls were whitewashed and the floor was covered with faded blue and white tiles. Rays of light from the waning day filtered into the room through the glazed windows and open shutters.

"There you are at last!" said a woman's voice.

Hanus pulled Jonah over to the voice. "My dear, I have brought someone home with me."

"Oh?" said the young woman. The firelight danced on red highlights in her hair.

"Jonah, this is my daughter, Isabel."

"I am glad to meet you," said Jonah. He could feel his face turning red.

Isabel glanced up from her work. She gave a start when she saw Jonah and put down her tools. "Father, can I speak with you?"

"Of course, child."

"Alone?"

"I'll wait outside," said Jonah.

Jonah walked outside and closed the door softly behind him. He could hear father and daughter talking.

"Father, why did you bring that boy here?"

"Why not? He seems like a good boy."

"But Father. He is Jewish."

"How do you know?"

"He is wearing the yellow circle on his jacket."

Jonah looked down at his jacket. *I'd better leave*, he thought. *This doesn't sound good*.

"I did not notice," said the clockmaker dryly. "So? Does that make him any worse than you or me?"

"No," said Isabel. "Just different."

"And do people not fear me as well because *I* am different?"

"Yes, Father, but …"

"Say no more," insisted Hanus. "Call the boy in and treat him like a guest."

"Yes, Father."

"Jonah, come in," said Isabel, holding the door open. "I need to finish my work. Then we will have supper."

Hanus sat down on a chair near the fireplace and held his hands out to the fire.

Jonah followed Isabel to the table under the window where she picked up her work. Tiny bits of metal were scattered on the surface. "What are you doing?"

"This? I am making a chain for *fusées*." She tilted her head. "It is a job they let women do. They say we are better at the delicate work than men."

"Fusées?"

"Yes. To control …"

"… the springs in small clocks." The words popped out of his mouth.

"How did you know that?" Hanus asked.

"I've been interested in clocks for a long time."

Hanus stood up. "Are you a spy? Or a thief?" he asked in a shaking voice. "Why have you come here?"

Jonah could not answer. The words choked in his throat. He wanted to cry out, *Yes, I am a thief!*

"Leave the boy alone, Father," said Isabel. "He is no spy."

"Well, all right." Hanus shrugged and sat back down. He seemed lost in his thoughts for several minutes, and then said, "Isabel, you work too hard!"

"There is nothing wrong with that!" Isabel answered. "If you waste an hour, it is like wasting a thousand!"

Hanus turned towards Jonah. "Since her mother died of the plague three years ago, she has been taking care of me. When I die —"

"Hush, Father!" said Isabel.

"When I die," Hanus repeated, "she will probably go into a convent. I want her to marry, but she refuses. She is already eighteen — almost too old to get married."

"Humph!" said Isabel, getting up from her workbench. She rubbed the back of her neck. Then, taking a taper from the fire, she lit a candle in the brass candlestick.

"Enough, Father!" Isabel placed bread and cheese on the table. "Come now, both of you. Sit down and eat." From a pot hanging over the fire, she ladled a thick bean soup into bowls.

When Jonah had finished eating, he stood up. "Thank you, but I must go now." *I have to look for Toby,* he thought. *Maybe he's wandering the streets. Maybe he's in trouble.* His stomach churned at the thought.

Hanus raised his head. "Jonah?"

"Yes?"

"Do you have a place to sleep tonight?"

"No," Jonah said softly.

"Then stay here. Tomorrow you may see the clock with me again."

Jonah sat down. He suddenly felt so tired he could hardly keep his eyes open. "Thank you. I would like that." He let Isabel lead him to a pallet by the fire.

"Tomorrow," he mumbled. "Tomorrow." Then he fell fast asleep.

On the way to the clock tower the next day, Jonah looked for Toby among the crowds of hurrying people. He was careful to avoid stepping on the stinking garbage in the street and the contents of chamber pots people threw out of their windows. His heart raced with excitement when he entered the clock room again.

"What do you know about clocks, Jonah?" asked Hanus, groping for his stool.

"I know you need to have a source of energy." Jonah guided him to the stool.

Hanus looked surprised. "Right. And where does that come from in *my* clock?"

"From the weights?"

"Right again! The weights pull gradually down while the verge and foliot regulate the energy."

"That's called the escapement?"

"Clever boy! Using a series of gears connected to the hands on the face of the clock, we can show what time it is."

"I like to look at your clock from the street."

"What is your favourite part?"

"When the figure of Death comes out and when the rooster crows."

Jonah heard a change in the rhythm of the gears, and saw the movement of the figures of the twelve apostles as they began their rotation to the front. The bell rang the fifth hour.

"It's a wonderful clock," sighed Jonah, after he had taken his hands away from his ears.

"Yes. Well, it is nice to be appreciated." Hanus sighed and stood up. "Time to go; Isabel will be worried."

Jonah followed Hanus down the stairs. "I'll take you home."

"Thank you. You are a good boy." Hanus put his hand on Jonah's shoulder.

Dad used to put his hand on my shoulder like that. The memory made Jonah ache. *I wish I could see him again, to make things right between us*. He straightened his shoulders. *Meanwhile, I still have to find Toby.*

They began to walk along the narrow street, their steps marking steady time like the great wheels of the clock. Light and shadow danced on the paving stones. The street was deserted except for a few people hurrying home to supper.

On the other side of the street, a man was keeping pace with them. No one seemed to notice him, even though he wore a sweatshirt and khaki pants. Jonah smelled the tobacco from his pipe. It was the Stranger!

"Hanus, will you wait here for a moment please?" Jonah said.

"Yes. But why?"

"I can't explain," said Jonah. "But I'll be right back."

Just as Jonah was about to cross the street, a gang of boys came running around the corner. "Hey, look!" shouted the boy in front.

"A Jew!" said another one.

Jonah's heart sank. He looked up and down the street. *Maybe I can run away,* he thought. *But how can I leave Hanus?*

"He's wearing the yellow circle," cried a third boy.

"Don't let him get away," said the leader.

"Jonah, what is going on?" called Hanus.

"Stay out of this, old man!" the leader said.

Jonah felt Hanus's fingers tighten on his shoulder. He raised his stick and started to wave it about. "Go away or I will call the police!" He brandished his stick again, but swished only empty air.

"Think they'll care? About that piece of garbage?" The leader grabbed the stick from Hanus, cracked it in two over his thigh, and threw the pieces behind him. Jonah could hear them clatter on the stones like the bones of a skeleton. The bullies closed in on Jonah and Hanus.

"Hold the Jew," ordered the leader. Two boys grabbed Jonah and held his arms down. Jonah tried to kick them, but they held his arms tightly while another boy punched him in the stomach.

One of the boys pushed Hanus hard against a nearby door and Hanus fell down. "Take that, Jew-lover!" Hanus tried to get up but the boy pushed him down again.

"Leave us alone!" Hanus gasped. He groped wildly, trying to push against his attacker. "Run!" he croaked.

Jonah struggled, but couldn't free himself from their tight grip. The bullies were pressing against him from all sides. He raised his arms to cover his head. Still they beat him on his shoulders, his arms, his face. He tried to hit back, but there were too many of them. He tasted blood. His head was throbbing. His stomach was aching. Lights spun wildly behind his eyes. Then there was nothing but blackness.

"Jonah? Are you okay?"

"What happened?" Jonah mumbled. He was lying on a bed. The light from a candle hurt his eyes and his head was pounding. He tried to open his eyes but they were swollen almost shut. "Toby?" His relief was almost more than he could bear.

"Yep. It's me."

"Where were you?"

"I came here a few hours ago." Toby smiled shakily. "I've been looking for you all this time."

"Me too." Jonah paused. "How did you find me?"

"I heard some boys fighting in the street, saw you in the middle of the action, and then a bunch of people stopped the fight." He grinned. "I figured you needed protecting!"

"Thanks. I did." Jonah's heart started beating wildly and he sat up with a start. He groaned as a sharp pain hit him behind his eyes. "Where's Hanus? Is he all right?"

"He's okay. We're at his place. His daughter found us on the street. She called the police, but the bullies ran away before the police could catch them."

Jonah lay back down. "Every part of my body hurts."

"You don't look so good, either."

"Now, what is all this talking?" said Isabel. She carried linen cloths and a bowl of warm water towards the bed. "This will make you feel better." She began to wash Jonah's face and hands.

Jonah started to blush. *I hope she won't touch me anywhere below the neck.* "Thank you. I feel much better now," he said hastily. "You can stop now."

"Thank you for helping my father." There were tears in Isabel's eyes. "You saved his life."

Don't be grateful, Jonah thought. *It was my fault the bullies attacked him in the first place.* "How is he?"

"He is resting." Isabel put the bowl on the table, picked up a bucket, and opened the door. "I must get more water. Then I will cook a healing broth."

She smiled. "Thank you again." She shut the door softly behind her.

"Toby, listen," Jonah whispered. "We need to talk."

Toby sat down on a stool next to Jonah.

"It's time to go. I don't want to get them into any more trouble." *I'll miss them and I wish I could talk more with Hanus about his clock.*

Toby nodded.

"I'm going to wind the watch now," said Jonah. "Try to stay with me this time."

"I'll do my best." Toby grinned. "Yahoo! Let's go to the next adventure!"

Jonah wound the watch. From far in the distance, he could hear Hanus's clock chiming in the town square.

7

LONDON, ENGLAND

1728

"Jonah, wake up!"

Jonah groaned. He was lying on a hard bed.

"Jonah, wake *up*!" said Toby. "Mr. Graham will be angry if you're late."

"Go away," said Jonah, pulling the thin blanket up to his chin.

"Come on," said Toby. "Get up!"

"Go away." Jonah tried to move further down the bed. *I don't want to get up,* he thought. *I don't want to be somewhere else besides home.*

Just then, Jonah felt cold water soaking his hair. He leaped out of bed. His blanket was sopping wet. "What did you do that for?" Jonah sputtered.

"I had to," said Toby, pretending to be sorry. He looked at Jonah, then at the wet blanket, and back at Jonah. He was holding an empty pitcher in his hands. His eyes shone with mischief.

Jonah chuckled. "I suppose that *was* pretty funny." He grabbed the pitcher and pretended to pour water over Toby's head. "Until I do the same thing to you!"

Toby smiled back at Jonah. "You know, sometimes funny things happen when a person travels into the past."

"Where are we?" Jonah asked, drying his face with a towel. "And who's Mr. Graham?"

"We're in London. Mr. Graham is a clockmaker."

"A clockmaker? Yay!"

Toby grinned. "I thought you'd like that." He placed the pitcher beside a bowl on a corner table. "I got here yesterday."

"Yesterday?"

"Yeah."

"What did Mr. Graham say?"

"That our father sent us here to be his new apprentices."

"What year is it?"

Toby straightened his back and pretended to unroll a piece of parchment. He announced, "Hear ye! Hear ye! We welcome you to the city of London, capital of the glorious British Empire, ruled by his Majesty King George II, in the year of our Lord 1728."

"1728! That explains it." Jonah stopped wiping his face. "You know, I've been thinking."

"That's a change!"

"Shut up and listen!"

"Speak, oh older and wiser one," said Toby, bowing low to the ground.

"The more we go forward, the more out of synch we get," said Jonah. "Have you noticed?"

"You mean, like we keep getting separated for longer and longer times?"

"Right."

"I've been trying not to think about it." Toby brightened. "So why don't we have some breakfast instead?" As he turned to leave, he said, "If you don't come down right now, I'll come back and pour more water on your head!"

Jonah threw his pillow at Toby, who shut the door hastily behind him. He heard Toby sing "Food, Glorious Food!" as he ran down the stairs.

Jonah walked over to the attic window. The slanted rooftops and smoking chimneys of London seemed to fill the sky. The foul smells of garbage and sewage wafted up from the street. Flocks of pigeons were everywhere, filling the air with their coos and the eaves with their droppings.

On the sidewalk below, a man was standing in the shadows. Smoke curled up from his pipe, but Jonah could see his bushy white hair, his sweatshirt and khaki pants, and a pair of sneakers on his feet. It was the Stranger! Jonah leaned out the window and waved at the man. He waved back at Jonah and beckoned him to come down.

Just then, some people hawking their wares blocked the Stranger from Jonah's view.

"Warm bread and rolls! Warm bread and rolls!"

"Milk! Cream! Butter!"

"Fresh eggs! Fresh eggs!"

By the time the sellers had moved on, the Stranger

had disappeared.

The hawkers' cries reminded Jonah that he was hungry. He walked down the stairs and into the kitchen. It was a bright sunny room with lace curtains on the windows and a gleaming wooden floor.

A woman whom he supposed was Mrs. Graham was cutting thick slices of bread which she slathered with butter. She wore a low-cut cotton dress with wide sleeves. Her brown curly hair peeked out from under a lace cap. She looked up at Jonah. "What a sleepyhead you are, boy. Sit down and eat something."

Mr. Graham looked up from his breakfast. He wore a white shirt with a muslin neck cloth, knee breeches, white stockings, and buckled shoes. He had a rather large nose, thin lips, and kindly eyes that looked at Jonah from under thick eyebrows. His fingers were long and delicate.

"You're the other new boy, I gather," Mr. Graham said. "Jonah, is it?"

"Yes, sir."

"Well, go ahead. Eat."

"Thank you, sir."

"The porridge is delicious," Toby whispered. "Especially if you put milk and brown sugar on it."

"No sand in the bread?"

"Nope," said Toby, chewing on a thick slice of bread and butter.

A clock on the mantel chimed eight o'clock. "Let's go, boys," said Mr. Graham. "Time to get to work."

Jonah and Toby followed Mr. Graham to the workshop that fronted the street. Everywhere Jonah looked, he saw clocks — long case pendulum clocks on the floor; mantel clocks on shelves. Their wooden cases glowed with polish; their faces shone in the sunlight streaming in through the window. Glass-fronted display cases held watches and various measuring instruments.

"Now then," said Mr. Graham. "Here is your work today." He pointed to an old pendulum clock lying on the worktable in the middle of the room. "The owner of this clock says it is losing too much time — five minutes a day." Mr. Graham shrugged. "Now, that is not too bad, considering that some clocks lose even more than that. But if we give it a good cleaning, that should make it right."

For the next few hours, they took the clock apart and placed each separate wheel, cog, and screw in order on the table. *I used to do this very thing at home,* Jonah thought. *But now it isn't a hobby. It's for real.*

"Jonah, pay attention to your work!" Mr. Graham scolded. "You will never learn your trade with your head in the clouds!"

"Sorry, Mr. Graham," mumbled Jonah.

The clocks in the shop all began to ring or chime or strike the noon hour. Mr. Graham looked at the boys. "Shall we see if Mrs. Graham has made some of her excellent steak and kidney pie for dinner?"

"Yes, sir!" said Toby.

"Kidneys?" Jonah whispered. "Yuk!"

The clocks in the Fleet Street shop were chiming ten o'clock the next morning when a man opened the door. He wore a long brown coat with numerous buttons over a dark waistcoat, brown breeches, and mud-spattered boots. He took off his three-cornered hat and held it in one hand; in the other, he carried a large leather case.

"Is this the shop of Mr. George Graham, the clockmaker?" the man asked.

"Yes, sir," said Toby.

"May I have a word with him, please? Tell him it's John Harrison come to see him."

"Right away, sir." Toby slid off his stool and went to look for Mr. Graham.

"Won't you sit down, Mr. Harrison?" said Jonah. He pointed to a chair near the door. *I read something about a John Harrison in one of my books. What was it again?*

"Thank you, boy," said the man, sitting on the very edge of the chair. He looked as if he might bolt out the door at any moment. He patted his hair, pulled at the sleeves of his coat, and fiddled with the lace cuffs on his shirt. He crossed his legs, uncrossed them, and crossed them again.

"Here he is, sir," said Toby.

"Good morning," said Mr. Graham. "How may I help you?"

The man stood up, transferred his hat to the hand holding the case, and shook Mr. Graham's hand as if it were a water pump.

"A pleasure, sir. A pleasure," said Harrison.

"Welcome to my shop," Graham said. "What can I do for you?"

"Sir, my name is John Harrison. And I have a business proposition for you." He released Graham's hand. His hat fell on the floor and he bent down to pick it up.

Graham pointed to two chairs. "Let us sit down, shall we?"

"Thank you, sir." The two men sat down and Harrison hugged his case tightly to his chest. "Mr. Halley, the Astronomer Royal, sent me to you."

"Edmund Halley? Why, I've just finished making a quadrant for him." Graham looked puzzled. "And why did he send you to me, pray?"

"Well, sir, he said if you didn't listen to me, the Board of Longitude wouldn't either."

Graham looked at Harrison's shabby clothes. "Quite right." Graham paused again. "Now, my dear Mr...?"

"John Harrison!" said Jonah. "I've heard of him."

Harrison looked astonished. "Me? A poor carpenter?"

"Don't interrupt, boy," said Graham. "And don't you have work to do?"

"Yes, sir," said Jonah. He began to clean one of the gear wheels of the clock. He longed to hear the men's conversation and moved his stool closer. Toby was busy drawing a picture of Mr. Harrison.

Harrison spoke in a low voice. "I've come to tell you about my idea for solving the longitude." He looked down at the floor. "And I need your help."

"The longitude?" Mr. Graham looked skeptically at Harrison. "But it has been fourteen years since Queen Anne offered the prize of £20,000! No one has come even close to claiming it, although Lord knows, many have tried."

Jonah gaped at Mr. Graham. He remembered something he had read in one of his books about the history of clocks. The prize was equivalent to over two million dollars in twenty-first century money!

Graham shook his head. "Our ships have been travelling the high seas for over two hundred years, and sailors still have no way of calculating their exact position."

"Mr. Graham, I'm sure I'm on the right track!" said Harrison. He stood up and began to pace back and forth. "The situation is getting quite desperate. More and more ships get lost, marooned, or wrecked.

"Countless men have died as a result of ship-wrecks. Drowned corpses lie bloating on the beaches of the Old World and the New." Harrison paused to take a breath. "That's why sailors must know where they are; that's why finding the longitude will make the difference between life and death."

Toby started singing under his breath, "It Was Sad When That Great Ship Went Down."

Jonah elbowed him. "Be quiet, will you? I want to hear what they're saying!"

Graham shook his head. "Boys nowadays have no manners."

"I understand," said Harrison. "I have boys of my own."

Toby kept humming the tune while he drew another picture, this one of a sailing ship.

"Look here, man," said Graham. "Everybody wants to win the prize, not to mention the fame. There have been many crackpot schemes. Why should I believe you?"

"I'm a clockmaker. Same as you. And the clocks I make are the most accurate in England — even more accurate than yours, if I may say so."

Graham frowned. "More accurate than mine?"

"Yes sir. Why, I have made a clock with wooden movements and gear wheels that keeps time within one second per month."

"One second per month? But that is impossible!"

"No, sir, it is not impossible. I have done it."

Graham stared at his visitor in amazement. "I would like to hear more about your clock, Mr. Harrison. And about your solution for the longitude."

"I'll show you, sir, but only you." Harrison lowered his voice. "I don't want anyone to steal my ideas."

Graham crossed his arms. "Mr. Harrison, I am a clockmaker, not a thief." His face softened. "But I do understand how desperate you must feel."

Graham walked to the door. "Elizabeth!"

Mrs. Graham, wiping her hands on a towel, came to the door. "Why are you shouting at me like a hawker at the market?"

"Elizabeth, this is Mr. John Harrison. He's a clockmaker from …?"

"Barrow-on-Humber," said Harrison.

"Yes. Quite. I would like to invite him for dinner." He turned toward Harrison. "Of course, if you agree?"

"It would be my pleasure."

"Good." Graham rubbed his hands together. "Now we can talk."

For the rest of the day and into the evening, Jonah listened as the two men discussed and argued about clocks and clock making. They stopped only long enough to eat dinner.

They talked about pendulums. They talked about escapements too — Graham about his "deadbeat" escapement; Harrison about his "grasshopper" escapement. It was the most fascinating talk Jonah had ever heard and he wished it could go on forever.

And something more — Jonah remembered what he'd read in his books. Harrison's watch, which he called a "chronometer," was worth more than a king's treasure. It would save people's lives!

Finally, Harrison told Graham the purpose for his visit. "I need you to make an accurate watch for me, according to my designs." He patted his case. "I've brought them with me." Harrison wagged his finger. "Soon we won't have to look at the stars for our position on earth. It is *time* that will tell us where we are!"

"By Jove, I believe you are right!" said Graham. "It is just as I suspected. Those foolish astronomers have been going about it the wrong way!"

"Will you make the watch for me then?"

Graham nodded. "I promise I will do my utmost for you."

Harrison handed the case to Graham, as if he were saying goodbye to a beloved child. "Here are my plans. Guard them with your life!"

"Have no fear, my good man. I shall."

"The evening grows late." Harrison stood up. "I have imposed on your hospitality long enough." He put his crumpled hat on his head and headed towards the door. Just before leaving, he turned back to say, "If I do get the longitude prize, it will be because people like you believed in me."

Graham stared after the departing figure of John Harrison and shook his head. "Well, boys, this has been quite a day."

"Wake up, Jonah!" Toby was shaking Jonah, who had been in a deep sleep.

"Leave me alone," Jonah mumbled. "Or are you going to dump water on me again?"

"There's a noise downstairs," Toby whispered. "In the shop."

Except for the moonlight seeping in through a crack in the shutters, the room was dark. "Go back to sleep. It's probably just mice. Or rats."

"Rats?" Toby shivered. "I hate rats!"

"Sorry. Just joking."

"Come on, Jonah. I hear voices."

"Voices?"

"Yeah. Will you get up?"

"All right, already!" Jonah put on his shirt and

pants. He slipped his feet into his shoes. "Wait a minute. I have to light a candle."

"And then what?"

"I don't know. I'm making this up as I go along."

"Right. Your usual plan."

"Do you have a better idea?"

"I guess not."

The boys tiptoed down the stairs, along the hall, and stood outside the door of the shop.

"Hurry up, Bill," said a man's deep voice from the other side of the door. "We have to find Harrison's plans before anyone hears us."

"Don't rush me, Tom," said another man with a higher voice. "These things 'ave to be done careful like."

"It's supposed to be in some kind of case."

Why are thieves looking for Harrison's plans? Jonah wondered. *And who am I to be catching thieves, when I'm one myself?*

"Got it," said Bill. "It's over 'ere."

"Grab it and let's go."

"Wait a minute. Don't you think we oughta take a little something for our trouble?"

"Why not? I fancy a nice pocket watch meself, like a gentleman wears."

Toby leaned over and whispered in Jonah's ear, "Come on. We've got to stop them." He straightened up and turned toward the door.

"Wait a minute!"

But Toby had already pushed open the door and was walking towards the men. "Not so fast," he squeaked. "You can't take that!"

"What the …?" It was Tom, the man with the deep voice.

"I said you can't take it," Toby repeated.

"Or you'll do what, boy?" Tom advanced towards Toby.

"I'll … I'll …"

"We'll call the police," said Jonah. His legs were shaking as he walked over to Toby.

"Another boy, eh?" said Bill, towering over the two.

"And what'll *you* do to stop me?" Tom was holding Harrison's leather case in his hand.

Jonah tried to grab the case from Tom, but Tom snatched his hand away. Then Bill cuffed Jonah on the head.

"Don't!" Toby kicked Bill's leg. "Leave him alone!"

"Leave *him* alone!" Jonah kicked Bill on the other leg.

"Stupid boys!" hissed Tom. "You should mind your own business!" He pulled a knife from his belt. "Grab 'em, Bill."

"Got 'em!" Bill yanked the boys by the hair and wrapped his arms around them. Jonah struggled but the man's huge hands were like bear paws, choking and smothering him.

"Tie 'em up, back to back," ordered Tom. He stood over the boys. His breath smelled of onions and rotten teeth. "Don't give us no trouble, if you know what's good for you." He looked around. "Use that chain, the one on the table there."

"Sit down," growled Bill. He pushed Toby and Jonah down on the chairs and fastened a thin chain tightly around their chests. *It's a fusée,* Jonah thought. *I remember when Isabel was working on them.*

"C'mon," said Tom. "Grab the stuff. Let's get out of here!" The men closed the door behind them. Jonah could hear the sound of their heavy boots running down the street.

"Now what?" Toby asked.

"I don't know. Let me think."

"Okay, Einstein."

"Sorry," said Jonah. "I'm not very good at this time travel business."

"I guess it's something you learn as you go along."

"You know what, Toby?"

"What?"

"You're not such a bad guy to have along on a trip."

"Even through time?"

"Especially through time."

"Can I sing my 'Brothers' song now?"

"No way!"

"Jonah?"

"What?"

"I'm hungry."

"What else is new?" Jonah smiled. He looked around the workshop. "Look, if we slide our chairs on the floor together, we can get to the workbench. There's a wire cutter there. Teamwork, right?"

"Let's go," said Toby.

When they reached the table, they leaned over together until Jonah could grab the wire cutter between his stiff fingers. Sweat poured into his eyes as he worked to cut the fusée. At last, after what seemed like hours, they were free.

"That's better!" Toby massaged his shoulders and neck. Jonah rubbed his hands together and stretched his fingers.

"We need to get out of here!" said Toby. "Those men might come back."

"I have to do something first." Jonah found a pen, bottle of ink, and a piece of paper on Mr. Graham's desk. He wrote a note and explained what had happened. "There, I'm done."

"Wait. I want to do one more thing." Toby picked up the pen and drew a picture of the two thieves.

"I guess art comes in handy once in a while," said Jonah, pushing Toby on the shoulder.

Toby made a face and pushed him back.

"It's time to go," said Jonah. "I wonder where we'll end up next time."

"I hope it's home," said Toby.

"Me too."

As Jonah wound the watch, all the clocks in Mr. Graham's workshop began to ring the hour.

8

PLYMOUTH, CONNECTICUT

1806

Jonah stood in front of a shop in a village nestled among rolling hills. He heard the ticking of the watch and felt its weight, heavy around his neck. He wore a cotton shirt, brown vest, and knee breeches. On his feet were leather shoes.

Where am I now? And where's Toby? Jonah felt sick to his stomach with panic and worry. *I've got to do something! Maybe Toby is in the shop.* He knocked on the door.

"Yes? What is it?" said the man who opened the door.

"I'm looking for my brother. Did he come by this way earlier?"

The man gazed up and down the road. "There's been no boy come this way but you. Are you lost?"

Jonah gulped. "Yes. I am." *If you only knew how lost I really am.*

"And hungry too, I wager."

Jonah nodded.

"What's your name?"

"Jonah."

"Well, come in, Jonah," said the man. "My name is Eli Terry. You can sit down on the stool over there. I'll be with you in a few minutes."

The room was about twenty feet square, with a low-beamed ceiling and plastered walls. Jonah knew immediately that it was a clock-making shop, for various tools were scattered on the bench: calipers, dividers, and files.

Eli Terry walked over to two men standing near the workbench.

One of the men said, "Mr. Terry, as I was saying, I'm Edward Porter and this is my brother, Levi." Edward Porter was tall and thin and spoke as if he were used to people listening to him. He wore a long coat over his shirt, a vest, and breeches. Mud-splattered boots were on his feet. "We've come all the way from Waterbury to talk to you. Just listen again to what Levi has to say."

"I don't know as that's going to help," said Eli. "You can talk till the cows come home, but I still think your idea is plain harebrained!" He looked sharply at the two men. "I've just started to get on my feet these last few years after building the new shop. And now you expect me to risk it all again?"

Jonah moved his stool a little closer to the men. They were so engrossed in their conversation they didn't notice him.

"We know it might sound crazy," said Levi Porter. "That's why we've come to you." He was puffing on a long clay pipe.

"Humph. Do I look crazy to you?" asked Eli, pressing his thin lips together. He was a short man and had to bend his head back to look at the Porter brothers.

"That's not what I meant," said Levi. He took the pipe out of his mouth and waved it in the air. "Tell him, Edward."

"He meant," said Edward Porter, "we think you're just the man for the job. You've got a reputation in Connecticut for finishing a task once you start it."

"And you're not afraid to take a risk," added Levi.

"Look," said Eli. "I like to keep an open mind about things, just like the next man." He pointed towards several high-back, wooden chairs on the other side of the room. "I still can't figure how you two, a minister and a button-maker, think you can turn a profit on clocks. But let's sit down over there and we can talk it over."

"Much obliged." They took off their hats and coats and hung them on pegs on the wall. They made their way around the tooth-cutting machines in the centre of the room and sat down.

"Jonah?" Eli said.

"Sir?"

"You'd best go up to the house and get us some cider." He paused. "And tell Mrs. Terry we might be having us some guests for supper. Including you." He glanced over at his visitors and said in a low voice, "Looks like this might be a long talk."

Jonah walked out of the shop, up a dirt path, and towards a small house. The trees behind the house covered the nearby hills like a thick green blanket. The house was made of wood, weathered to grey, with two windows on each side of the front door. The panes of glass in the windows were small, but the sunlight shone on them like sparkling gems. The roof was made of wood shingles and sloped steeply on both sides.

Mrs. Terry looked up from stirring a pot of soup on the stove when Jonah entered the kitchen. Pots, pans, baskets, drying herbs, strings of onions and garlic crowded the walls or hung from hooks on the ceiling. The fire in the fireplace crackled and snapped.

A handsome clock sat on the mantelpiece. The brass on the clock shone and the pendulum made a comforting ticking sound. Three young boys were playing with carved wooden animals under the trestle table while an older girl sat at the table and shelled peas.

"And who are you?" Mrs. Terry's brown eyes smiled kindly at Jonah. She wore a long, printed cotton dress and a cap on her head.

"My name is Jonah. I'm looking for my brother."

"Your brother? Now where might he be?"

"I wish I knew!" Jonah swallowed hard and tried to hold back his tears.

"There now, I'm sure he'll turn up. There aren't many places a boy can hide in our town."

Jonah nodded and took a deep breath. "Mr. Terry sent me to fetch cider and mugs. Two men have come from Waterbury to talk to him. And Mr. Terry says they might be staying for supper."

"I guess I'd better put some more potatoes in the soup," Mrs. Terry said. "And more carrots, too."

"Mama," said the girl, "who do you suppose those men are?"

"I'm wondering that myself, Anna," answered Mrs. Terry. She poured cider into a jug, took three pewter mugs from their hooks in the cupboard, and put them on the table. "And I guess I should add more water to the soup, too," she said.

She reminds me of the chickens in front of the house, pecking away at one thing or another all day long, Jonah thought.

"Sit down, Jonah," Mrs. Terry said. "Have some cornbread and a glass of milk. Who knows how long the men will be."

Jonah looked over his shoulder. "I should be getting back."

"It won't hurt to sit for a while."

"Thanks, ma'am." Jonah sat down across from Anna at the long table. The sun coming through the window shone on her blond pigtails.

Mrs. Terry sat down at the end of the table and began to peel potatoes. Just then, one of the boys let out a yell, pulled himself out from beneath the table, and ran sobbing to his mother. She picked the toddler up and hugged him tightly.

"Eli Junior, stop teasing James!" she scolded, as she looked under the table at her oldest boy.

"Ma, I wasn't!" said Eli Junior. "It was Henry. Not me."

"Wasn't me," countered Henry. "Was you."

"Wasn't!"

"Was!"

"Wasn't!"

"Was!"

"Quiet!" demanded their mother. "Or I'll give you both a whack on your backsides you won't forget!" She put James down and he immediately crawled back under the table. "Now hush up."

"Yes, Ma," said Eli Junior and Henry together.

"I'll be glad when Eli Junior starts school in the fall, that's for sure," said Mrs. Terry, as she finished peeling the potatoes. "It's time he had some learning in him. Then maybe he'll stay out of mischief!"

"I wish I could keep going to school," said Anna wistfully.

"You've already learned your letters and numbers. That's enough for a girl of ten." Mrs. Terry began to cut the potatoes into small chunks and put them in a bowl of water.

"But Ma …"

"Eunice!" called a voice from outside. "Where's that Jonah gone off to?"

"He's right here, sitting in my kitchen!" said Mrs. Terry. "And you don't have to shout!"

The door flew open and Eli Terry stomped into the room. "Jonah, I asked you to bring the cider."

"Sorry." Jonah stood up and brushed cornbread crumbs off his breeches.

"Don't be in such a hurry, Eli," said Mrs. Terry. "We were just having us a little talk."

"That's all well and good," said Eli, "but I don't like to keep my visitors waiting."

"Well, the cider's sitting right there." Mrs. Terry gave Jonah a nudge. "And when you're done talking, you can come for supper. It'll be ready in about an hour."

Eli nodded. "Come along, boy. I'll bring the pitcher; you bring the mugs."

The smoke from Levi Porter's pipe was curling around the ceiling beams when they returned to the workshop. Jonah sat back down on the stool.

"Like I was saying," continued Edward Porter. "When we heard how you use waterpower to drive the lathe and saws to make the wooden parts for your clocks —"

"That's what decided us," interrupted Levi. "That's the way of the future."

"I'm glad you think so," said Eli. He took a long iron rod from the fire, blew off the ashes, and thrust the red-hot end into the pitcher. There was a hissing sound and the scent of cinnamon, nutmeg, and cloves filled the air.

He poured the cider into the mugs and handed one to each of his guests. "The days of making only one clock at a time are long past. The trouble is, all I can make is about two hundred clocks a year."

"But that's more than any other clockmaker in the country!" said Edward.

"I tell you," said Levi, "there's a real demand for clocks. The frontier's opening up. Towns are getting bigger. The country's booming. People are looking for a bit of luxury."

"Everyone wants a clock," added Edward. "Even a poor farmer." He sipped his cider. "That's often the only nice thing the family owns."

"We aim to fill the needs of all those people," Levi said. "We figure we can sell four thousand movements for long case clocks if we can buy them cheaply enough." He chewed on the stem of his empty pipe. "We have peddlers who'll sell them for us, here in Connecticut and all the way out to Indiana, Illinois, and Kentucky. Even as far away as Missouri or Arkansas!"

"That's where you come in, Mr. Terry," said Edward.

"I was wondering about that," said Eli, taking a hard look at his guests. "Four thousand movements." He shook his head. "Why, that's more than all the clockmakers in the state have made in the past ten years!"

"True enough, Mr. Terry," said Edward. "But we think *you* can do it."

"We'll supply all the wood you'll need — oak and laurel — and we'll pay you hard cash," said Levi.

"Four dollars a movement when you're done," said Edward.

Jonah could almost hear Eli Terry doing the mental arithmetic.

"Wait a minute!" Eli said. "I'm charging twenty-five dollars a movement right now, including the brass dial. How do you expect me to lower my costs that much and still make a profit?"

"We're sure you can figure it out," said Edward. He drained his mug and looked longingly at the pitcher.

"There's one more thing," added Levi, tapping the ashes out of his pipe.

"What?" Eli asked.

"We need to have the movements ready within three years."

"Three years!" Eli shook his head. "Now I'm sure of it. *You're* the crazy ones!"

"It's the only way we figure we can make a profit," said Edward. "Before the competition catches on to our idea."

"Think about it," said Levi. "Talk it over with your wife, if you like. You can let us know in a few days."

The men looked at Eli, then at each other. They both stood up at the same time.

"Well, we'll be leaving now," said Edward, holding out his hand.

Eli extended his hand as if it didn't belong to him. He seemed a million miles away.

"Hope to hear from you soon," said Levi, shaking Eli's hand. "We're staying down the road. At Fenn's Tavern." The men began to put on their hats and coats.

"I'll think about your offer and let you know," said Eli.

Jonah scurried to open the door for the Porter brothers. He looked at their backs as they walked away down the muddy road. Their heads were close together and they were talking intently.

A man was walking along the road. He held a pipe in one hand and a violin case in the other. The Stranger looked at Jonah and smiled. He hurried towards Jonah and gestured for him to come out.

Jonah opened the door wider, but just then Eli Terry said, "Close that door, Jonah. You're letting in the flies."

Jonah turned. "Just a minute, Mr. Terry." But when Jonah looked back down the road, the Stranger had vanished. Reluctantly, he closed the door.

"Gosh darn!" Eli said. "I forgot to ask the Porters to stay for supper!"

That evening, the family was gathered around the kitchen fire. Mrs. Terry's knitting needles flashed over a pair of socks in time with the rocking of her chair. Anna was struggling with the tiny stitches on an embroidery sampler.

I wish my own family were like that, Jonah thought. He stared at the flames dancing in the hearth. *I wish I knew where Toby was!*

Eli Terry sat on a high-back chair by the fire. He was telling a story to his two older sons, who were lying on the hearthrug at his feet. Little James was asleep in the crib in his parents' room.

"So, Jack grabbed the giant's magic harp," Eli began, "ran to the beanstalk, and climbed down it as fast as his legs would carry him. All the while, the giant chased after him and bellowed in a voice like thunder. 'Fee! Fie! Foe! Fum!'" Eli Junior and Henry moved closer to each other.

"When Jack came home, he yelled, 'Ma! Get me the axe!' And do you know what Jack did then?"

"What?" asked the boys together.

"Why, he grabbed that axe and cut down the beanstalk close off at the root — chop, chop, chop."

"What happened then?" said Eli Junior.

"The giant fell headlong into the garden. And that fall killed the giant — dead as a doornail. As for Jack and his mother ..."

"They lived happily ever after," said Henry, with a satisfied sigh.

"Boys, high time you went to bed," said Mrs. Terry, putting down her knitting.

"But Ma!" pleaded Henry.

"Just one more story?" begged Eli Junior.

"Tomorrow's another day," said Mrs. Terry. "Come along now." She picked up a candlestick from the table and lit the candle with a taper from the fire.

"Good night, boys," said Eli.

"Good night, Pa," said both boys. They reluctantly followed their mother up the stairs leading to the attic. The light from the candle cast flickering shadows on the walls.

Eli picked up his newspaper, the *Hartford Connecticut Current*, but he stared at it without reading.

Anna yawned. "Pa, I'm going to bed, too."

"What? Oh, good night, dear."

"I guess I'll be going, too," said Jonah.

"Good night, boy."

Jonah lay down on his bed in the attic room. He watched the moonlight dancing on the ceiling. *I hope Toby found a safe place to stay, wherever he is.* He heard Mr. and Mrs. Terry talking in the room below.

"Eli?"

"Huh?"

"What did those men say to you today?"

Eli told Eunice what the Porter brothers had proposed. "Now, if I could just figure out how to do it!"

"Eli, if you can make two hundred clocks a year, you can make a thousand," said Eunice confidently. Jonah heard the faint clicking of her knitting needles and the creaking of the rocking chair.

"Easier said than done," said Eli. "For starters, I'll have to buy a bigger shop...."

"Near the river, I suppose? For the waterpower?"

"Yep ... And if I could rig a really big pulley, and connect it to the saws and the lathes ..."

"Then you'd be able to make a lot of parts at the same time, wouldn't you?"

It was quiet, except for small sounds — the ticking of the clock on the mantel and the squeaking of the floorboards as Eli paced the floor.

"Eunice, now suppose, just suppose, I had a machine that could make the same part over and over again ..."

"The same part?"

"The exact same part! Like gear wheels," Eli said excitedly. "Then the parts in one clock would fit any other of the four thousand clocks I make!"

"But that's a lot of parts. You'll need to get yourself more help." She paused. "And that would cost a lot of money."

"But the workers wouldn't have to know all about clock making. Just one or two jobs. They'd do them over and over again. Why, even a boy like Jonah could do it!"

"Eli, sit down. You're making me dizzy!"

"Eunice, it's never been done before, but I think it'll work!"

"Course it'll work."

"But what about the risk?" Eli said.

"The Porters said they'd give you some money to get started, didn't they?"

"They did say that."

"So, there you are. We'll manage just fine."

"Then you think I should do it?"

"I do. Now let's go to bed. That's enough excitement for one day!"

Later that night, Jonah woke up, coughing hard. His eyes watered and his stomach hurt. A grey haze blanketed everything. The air was thick with smoke and the acrid smell was in his nose, his mouth, his throat. He threw his quilt aside and jumped out of bed. *I've got to get out of the attic. And get the boys out, too!*

Jonah stumbled to their bed. "Henry! Eli Junior! Get up!" he shouted. "Hurry!" He shook them again and again until they woke up. The boys were coughing and crying, but were too afraid to move. *I've got to get us out of here!*

"Come on!" said Jonah. "Follow me!" He pulled their arms and led them, crawling, down the stairs and into the kitchen.

Anna was standing beside the table. She was coughing and rubbing her eyes. She didn't seem to know where she was. "Anna!" he gasped. "Take the boys outside!" He pushed them into her arms, yanked the door open, and shoved them all outside.

"Move away from the house," he warned. "I've got to get your folks out!" Staggering through the thick smoke, more by touch than by sight, he made his way to the Terrys' bedroom.

He pushed the door open and stumbled over to the bed. "Wake up, Mr. Terry," he said, shaking him. "Wake up!"

"Jonah? What's going on?" Eli croaked.

"Fire!" gasped Jonah. "You've got to get out of here!"

"James!" cried Mrs. Terry.

Mr. Terry picked the toddler up from his crib, and the Terrys stumbled out of the room together.

The thick smoke wrapped its arms around Jonah's body and smothered all his senses. He sank to the floor. He couldn't see; he couldn't breathe; he couldn't move. In desperation, he grasped the knob of the watch and made one quick turn. Then he passed out.

9

BANDORAN, IRELAND

1876

Jonah was standing in front of a train station. The name BANDORAN was etched in wood above the door.

He wore a linen shirt rolled to the elbows, tattered pants held up by a piece of rope, a bright red kerchief around his neck, and a cloth cap.

His head buzzed with questions. *I wish I could be like Merlin, the wizard in the King Arthur stories. People said Merlin knew the future as well as the past. My memories are starting to shred apart like a torn spider's web. And where's Toby? Will I ever see him again?*

Jonah stepped inside the station. A few rays of late afternoon sun filtered through the windows and lit up faded travel posters advertising places like Dublin and Belfast and London. A half-torn calendar on the wall showed the year was 1876.

A tall, bearded man stood at the ticket window. He wore a brown travelling cloak and a plaid hat on his head. He waved a thick book in the face of the stationmaster standing on the other side of the wicket.

"This is the *Official Irish Travelling Guide*," the man said. "Surely you canna argue agin' that?"

"No, but ..." The stationmaster pushed his glasses up to the bridge of his nose. He was a short, wiry man, with hair sticking out in unlikely places — his ears, his nostrils, his wrists.

"Look here. What is your name?" said the man.

"Mr. Ward," the agent replied.

"My name is Fleming." The man pointed at a page in his book. "Now Mr. Ward, it says here the train for Londonderry is supposed to leave at 5:35 p.m." He pulled a gold watch out of his waistcoat pocket, released the catch, and looked at the time. He shut the watch with a loud click. "It is only ten minutes past the hour. That leaves me twenty-five minutes to catch the train. Now, will you kindly sell me a ticket so I can get on that blasted train?"

"But Mr. Fleming, I've been tryin' to tell you. The train leaves at 5:35 but ..."

"But what?" Fleming looked like a bear that was ready to pounce on poor Mr. Ward.

"5:35 ... in the mornin'," said Mr. Ward, shrinking back.

Fleming looked stunned. "That canna be right. Here, man, look at the schedule." He handed the stationmaster the book.

Mr. Ward peered at the small print. "It's very sorry I am, sir," he said, shaking his head. "There *is* a mistake. You see, it's supposed to read 5:35 a.m., not 5:35 p.m. So, there you are," he said, handing the book back to Fleming.

"I canna believe this! Do you have any idea the trouble this will cause me?"

"I'm very sorry, sir. It's not my fault, nor the fault of our clocks," said Mr. Ward. He pointed to a large clock on the wall. "It keeps very accurate time. Made in London. Like all the clocks in all the train stations in the entire British Empire."

"Yes, I know all about that," said Fleming impatiently. "Eli Terry in America worked out how to mass produce them."

Eli Terry! Jonah thought. *I met him!* He sidled over to the men.

Mr. Ward began tidying up his desk. "No more trains are scheduled to leave this evening. And I must go now, or the missus will give me a talkin' to, sure enough."

"But … what am I to do now? My friends are waiting for me in Londonderry."

"You can send them a telegram, if you like."

"You have a telegraph line here?"

"Indeed we do," said Ward proudly. "I can send your message right away." He paused. "But I'd be much obliged if you'd be quick about it." He pointed to paper, pen, blotter, and ink bottle on the counter.

"Hurry to stand still," grumbled Fleming. He dipped the pen nib into the ink, wrote his message, blotted the ink, and gave it to Mr. Ward.

Mr. Ward counted the words. "That will be one shilling."

Fleming took a coin from his pocket and handed it to Mr. Ward.

"Thank you, sir." Jonah heard the clicking of the telegraph machine as Mr. Ward sent the message.

Fleming slumped down on a nearby chair. He stared at the dust motes dancing in the sun's rays coming through the dirty window.

Mr. Ward called over to Jonah. "Boy, come here a minute, will you?"

"Sir?" Jonah walked over to the ticket window.

"What's your name?"

"Jonah."

"Are you one of those travellers, those gypsies?"

What should I say? Jonah thought. *I'm a traveller, but not in the way the man means.*

"Another boy, a stranger, came by here yesterday."

"He did?" Jonah's heart started racing.

Mr. Ward nodded. "He wore the same clothes as you."

Jonah looked frantically around the station. "Where did he go?"

"I told him to go down to the river. Where the other gypsies were camped."

"But some people don't like gypsies," called Mr. Fleming. "They think they're thieves and make trouble."

Jonah shrank at the word "thief." *Mr. Fleming is more right than he knows.*

Mr. Ward shook his head. "Some of the men from the village ran them out of town last night."

"I've got to find him!" said Jonah. "He's my brother!"

"Hold on, boy," said Mr. Fleming. "He must be long gone by now."

"They were planning to go north. Towards Londonderry," said Mr. Ward.

"Why, I'm going that direction tomorrow," said Mr. Fleming. "You can go on the same train as I."

Jonah felt like crying. "I ... I don't have any money."

Fleming looked hard at Jonah. "Maybe you can earn the money for a ticket." He turned to Mr. Ward. "Is there a job you can give this boy?"

"As a matter of fact, there is." He pointed to a corner of the station. "There's a bucket with a mop over there. If you wash the floor tonight, that'll cover your fare."

"That's settled, then," said Mr. Fleming.

"Thank you, sirs," said Jonah. He gulped hard, grateful for the kindness of strangers.

Mr. Ward pointed to several people in the room. "All of them are waitin' for the mornin' train. I must be leavin' now." He tidied his desk, placed the unsold tickets in a drawer, and locked the drawer with a key. "Good night to you, sir," he said, tipping his cap in Fleming's direction. "See you in the mornin'."

"I might as well make myself comfortable," Fleming said, as he slouched back into his chair and took a cigar out of his pocket. He cut the end of the cigar with a small pair of scissors, took a match out of a box from his pants pocket, struck the match on the bottom of his shoe, and lit the cigar. He puffed several times until he was sure it was lit satisfactorily. He seemed lost in thought.

"I'll wash the floor now," Jonah said. He picked up the bucket and filled it with water from the well outside the station. He mopped the floor until he reached the bench where two young men were sitting. Each one had a battered suitcase at his feet.

"Excuse me," said Jonah.

"What do you want?" said one of the men.

"I need to wash the floor."

"Hey, Joe," said the second man.

"What?"

"Isn't that boy one o' them gypsies we run out of town yesterday?"

"He looks the part, right enough, Frank," said Joe. "I guess we missed one then, didn't we?"

"I guess so." The men stood up and grabbed Jonah's arms.

"Stop!" Jonah cried. "Let me go!"

The men began to drag him out of the station.

"Now what's this?" boomed a loud voice. It was Mr. Fleming. "What are you doing to the boy?"

"He's a thievin' gypsy, that's what!" said Joe.

"We know what to do with that kind, don't we now?" said Frank.

"You leave that boy alone or ..." said Fleming.

"Or you'll do what, old man?" said Joe.

Fleming clenched his fists and took a boxer's stance. The muscles bulged against the sleeves of his jacket. "Do you want to fight me?"

"Well now," said Joe, putting his hands up. "We didn't mean any harm, did we now?"

"None at all," said Frank, patting Jonah's shirt. "Just wanted to have a little fun, is all."

"Fine," said Mr. Fleming. "Go sit down over there and leave the lad alone."

The men shuffled back to the bench and spoke in low voices, glaring at Fleming from time to time.

"Thank you, Mr. Fleming," said Jonah.

"I can't stand narrow-minded people."

When Jonah had finished mopping the floor, Fleming pointed to the seat beside him. "You may as well sit down. I can see this will be a long night. Perhaps you'll make it shorter." He paused. "I was thinking about this country. We have so much wealth and talent. And then there are the railways."

"The trains are wonderful, sir!"

"Aye! But we still canna get a railway schedule right!" Fleming shook his head. "Enough of that. How old are you, lad?"

"Twelve years old."

"You know, I have a son about your age back home. You remind me of him." *Maybe that's why he's being so nice to me,* Jonah thought.

"Six years of schooling," mused Fleming. "That's as much as I had, come to think of it. Then I was apprenticed to Mr. John Sang in Kirkcaldy."

"Kirkcaldy?"

"Scotland. I learned my trade from him."

"Trade? But what do you do, sir?"

"I'm a surveyor."

"What's that?"

"I measure the land and prepare maps for builders and engineers."

"That must be wonderful," sighed Jonah.

"It is, indeed." Fleming had a faraway look in his eyes. "There was no better teacher than Mr. Sang. When I was finished learning everything I could, I left Scotland."

"And is it back to Scotland you're going to now, sir?"

Fleming relit his cigar, took a puff, and flicked the ash into the ashtray near his chair. "Back there? Nae, lad. I go to Londonderry, to visit friends. My home is in Canada now. Let me show you."

He reached into his leather case and took out paper and pencil. He began to draw a map as he continued to tell his story. "Canada. A better home a man couldna have. Eighteen years old I was when I left Scotland."

"I want ... I want ... to leave here!" Jonah blurted out. *I want so much to go home! But first I have to find Toby.*

"Do you now?" Fleming straightened his back and peered at Jonah. "And where would you go?"

"To Canada."

"I helped build the Canadian transcontinental railway, you know." Fleming frowned. "But there's one problem we haven't solved yet."

"What?"

"Time. We don't know how to show the difference between 5:35 in the afternoon and 5:35 in the morning! We need to know the precise time. On a clock. Or on a train schedule."

"What do you mean?"

Fleming lit his cigar again and puffed on it before answering. "You know how quickly a train moves?"

"No," said Jonah.

"Sometimes over forty miles an hour!" Fleming shook his head. "In the old days, before there were trains, every town and village had its own local time. It didn't matter, because horses moved slowly and you could adjust the time as you travelled along.

"Nowadays, trains move so fast that people get confused about the different local times." Fleming pointed his cigar at Jonah. "Why, did you know that the town of Buffalo has four different times?"

"Buffalo, New York?"

Fleming looked shrewdly at Jonah. "Indeed."

He stood up and began to pace back and forth. "People must know what time it is, in a clear, unmistakable way. Whether they're travelling in England or Ireland or Scotland or —"

"Canada!" said Jonah.

"Indeed, why not?" mused Fleming. "All of Canada. From coast to coast. And all of the United States, too. Maybe even … all of the world." Fleming seemed to have forgotten that Jonah was there.

Jonah stood up and walked out of the station. As he looked down the tracks, they seemed to beckon to him, like a leprechaun showing him the path to a pot of gold.

A man was riding his bicycle along the road towards the village. He was wearing a sweatshirt and khaki pants. He hummed a tune as his sneakers pushed the pedals. An old violin case was tipped precariously in the bicycle basket. It was the Stranger!

Jonah called out, "Wait! Stop!" but the man continued to ride away. Jonah ran after him but when he turned the corner, the Stranger had vanished.

All night long, Jonah tossed and turned, trying to get some sleep on the hard bench in the station. He was hungry, thirsty, and dirty. *I wish I had a toothbrush,* Jonah thought. *Mom always reminded me to pack a toothbrush. I wish I'd listened to her more.*

Fleming was lying on a bench, his bag under his head, his coat covering only part of his body. Cigar ash lay on the floor beneath him like the droppings of tiny mice. He groaned and slowly sat up. Jonah could almost hear his bones creaking.

Fleming stretched and gave a huge yawn, like a bear coming out of its cave after a long winter's sleep.

"Is there anything to eat or drink in this place?"

"I don't think so."

"Sit down, Jonah," Fleming said. "I've had an idea. Let me try it out on you."

Jonah sat down next to Fleming.

"Remember we were talking about this time problem?"

Jonah nodded.

"This is what I was thinking," Fleming said slowly. "Instead of a clock with twelve hours, think of one with twenty-four hours."

"Twenty-four hours?"

"Aye! You would count twenty-four hours, from midnight to midnight. Then there would be no confusion about time, no matter if it's day or night."

"But ... what would happen at 12 noon?"

"Simple! You just keep counting. For example, at 1:00 p.m., you add one hour to the 12. You would have thirteen o'clock, or 1300 hours!"

"And 8:00 p.m.?"

"Add 12 to it and you have ..."

"Twenty o'clock!"

"Aye! Or 2000 hours. I knew you were a canny lad!"

Jonah blushed. "Then at midnight, would the clock start all over again?"

"Aye! You see? Crystal clear! It will be a new way of telling time!"

"That's wonderful, sir!" said Jonah. "I'm sure it will work."

"Of course it will work. Not just here, but in the whole world! And then, if we could work out a system of time zones ..."

Just then, Mr. Ward walked into the room. "Five o'clock!" he announced.

"0500," whispered Fleming, winking at Jonah.

"The train for Londonderry will leave at 5:30!" Ward said.

"0530," said Jonah.

Fleming picked up his bag. "We'd better go outside."

With a great huffing and puffing and with smoke belching from its smokestack, the train arrived at the platform.

"Trains! Dirty, smelly, noisy creatures they are!" said Fleming. He held out his hand and Jonah shook it.

"Jonah, thank you for your help," said Fleming. "Now you'd better go get your seat in the third-class carriage."

"Thank you, sir," said Jonah. "I'll never forget you!"

Fleming took a pencil out of his pocket and jotted something in his notebook. "You seem like a good lad. If you ever come to Canada, I shall do what I can to get you started." He tore the piece of paper from the notebook and handed it to Jonah. "Here's my address. Remember. My name is Fleming. Sandford Fleming."

"Yes, sir!" Jonah shouted as he tipped his cap. "Thank you, sir!"

"Good lad!" Fleming grabbed his bag and walked up the steps into the train.

"All aboard!" shouted the conductor. Jonah hurried into the third-class carriage. The train rolled away with a massive turning of its iron wheels and a hissing of its engine.

The car was almost empty, except for the two men who had bullied him the day before. They sat a few rows behind Jonah.

Jonah stared out the window at the rolling hills and tried to ignore the men. He looked for the gypsies' campsite near the tracks, but the country had a stupefying sameness to it and he must have dozed off.

Jonah was jerked out of his sleep by a rough hand on his arm. Someone was shaking him and foul breath was blasting in his face. It was Joe from the station.

"Me and my friend were wonderin' what you're doin' on this train."

"I ... I'm looking for my brother."

"Bet he's a gypsy like you!" said Frank, who stood behind Joe.

"I'm not," Jonah said. "I'm —"

"You oughtn't to be on a train with respectable people," said Joe.

"Yeah. You oughta be where you belong," added Frank.

"Two brothers!" sneered Joe. "Probably the same, like two peas in a pod."

"We should help the poor boy find his brother," Frank said.

"O' course we should!"

Both men began to laugh but it was not a friendly laugh. Joe grabbed Jonah's arms while Frank grabbed his legs. Jonah kicked but they were too strong. They carried him along the aisle to the end of the car. Joe booted open the door and together they threw Jonah out of the moving train.

"Good riddance!" they shouted as the train carried them away.

The wind was knocked out of Jonah as he rolled down the stony embankment. He tasted dirt in his mouth while the hard earth scraped his elbows and knees. At last, he stopped rolling and came to rest at the bottom of a gully. He gulped air until at last he could breathe normally again.

His whole body felt like one large bruise. He sat up and looked around him. Birds were singing in the trees and he heard the gurgling of a brook. He limped to the edge of the brook, crouched down, and splashed water on his hands and face. It was then that he heard the music.

It was music such as he had never heard before — plaintive, haunting, free. Jonah made his way along the edge of the brook and followed the music as it beckoned to him.

All at once, he stumbled into a clearing. A group of people were sitting around an open fire. They were talking and playing cards. A woman was stirring the contents of a pot hanging over the fire. A man played the violin; another, a flute. Suddenly, the music stopped and everyone stared at Jonah. A young man stood up and walked over to Jonah.

"What is it you want here?" demanded the man.

"I … I'm looking for my brother."

The man advanced toward Jonah. "No strangers are allowed here. Now get out!" The man put his hands on Jonah's shoulders and pushed him back in the direction he had come from.

"No! Please wait!" cried Jonah. "I have to find him!"

"Felix! Stop!" a woman's voice said. "He is only a boy." A woman with a deeply lined face came to stand behind Felix. "Let him go."

Felix's face grew red as he looked at the others sitting around the fire. They shrugged and motioned him to sit down. "All right, Mother." He walked back to the fire and sat down. *He's not much older than I am,* Jonah thought.

The woman wore a full skirt and cotton blouse. With every movement, the necklace and bracelets she wore tinkled like music. "My name is Theresa. I am head of this camp." She put her hands on her hips. "What does your brother look like?"

"Like him, but more handsome," said a voice. Toby stepped out from behind the wagon and walked up to Jonah.

"Toby!"

"Jonah!"

The boys stared at each other for a moment, and then started talking at once.

"Where were you?"

"Where were *you*?"

"Here."

"There."

They hugged and laughed and began to play-fight and roll around on the ground until Theresa shouted, "Stop!"

The boys got up and stood sheepishly in front of Theresa.

"You are lost?" she asked.

"Yes," Jonah said.

"Then you will stay with us for the night. In the morning, we move to the next town and then you must leave."

"Thank you," said Jonah and Toby together.

Theresa pointed to the fire. "Come. Eat now."

Everyone sat down while Theresa ladled stew into metal bowls.

"This is good," whispered Toby, smacking his lips.

Jonah leaned towards Toby. "Yeah, if you like to eat bunnies."

"Bunnies?" Toby's spoon stopped halfway to his mouth.

"Don't worry. They say it tastes like chicken."

"I just lost my appetite."

Jonah grinned. "That's impossible."

The next morning, Theresa called Jonah over to the covered wagon. "Come, Jonah. I will read your fortune."

Jonah shook his head. "It's okay. I don't need to know the future." *I have enough to handle with the past.*

"You must come."

Jonah had the feeling that a person could not refuse anything Theresa wanted. He climbed onto the wagon and sat down on an old box opposite Theresa. She held his hand, looked at his fingers, and traced the lines along his palm.

"You are on a journey," Theresa said.

Oh, if you only knew, thought Jonah.

"Your journey is almost over. You have learned many lessons."

"Lessons?"

Theresa gazed at Jonah with deep, brown eyes. "You have done something wrong, but soon you will make it right."

Jonah pulled his hand away and stood up. "I think I'd better go now."

"Wait! I have more to tell you."

"No thanks. I've heard enough." He climbed down from the wagon and hurried over to where Toby was drawing on the ground with a stick.

He touched Toby on the shoulder. "Toby," he whispered.

"What?"

"Come on."

"Where?"

"Where do you think?"

"Home?"

"I hope so."

The two boys walked away from the gypsies' camp until they were alone.

"Now, Jonah?"

"Now. And Toby?"

"What?"

"Try to stay with me this time."

"I'll try."

Jonah wound the watch. As the light faded, he heard the neighing of a horse and the faint jingle of jewellry.

10

OTTAWA, CANADA

1958

"Remember what I told you, class. Stay together, and don't touch anything." Jonah was standing with a group of children outside a two-storey, rectangular building. He wore a plaid shirt, a pair of jeans with cuffs, and sneakers on his feet. He felt more comfortable than he'd been in a long, long time.

A large sign announced:

> National Research Council
> Division of Physics
> Ottawa, Canada
> Established 1951

"Are you the new boy in Mrs. Henderson's class?" whispered a girl next to Jonah. He nodded.

On her dress, the girl wore a nametag with the name DEBORAH. Underneath someone had scrawled, NOT DEBBIE.

Mrs. Henderson was talking in a high-pitched voice. "While we're waiting for Dr. Bailey, let's go over the things we learned in class."

The children groaned. A boy at the side of the group made a funny face and scratched under his arms like a monkey. It was Toby!

Jonah edged over towards Toby. *I don't want to lose him ever again.*

"Toby!" warned Mrs. Henderson. "Watch your manners, or you'll wait for us in the bus."

"Yes, Mrs. Henderson," said Toby. Under his breath, he muttered, "Old sourpuss!"

"Children, what is the most accurate clock in the world today?" Mrs. Henderson asked. Several hands shot up in the air. "Yes, Tammy?"

"An atomic clock."

"Good. And what kind of atoms are in an atomic clock?" Mrs. Henderson looked at the group. No one answered. "Jonah! Are you daydreaming?"

Toby gave Jonah a nudge and Deborah whispered, "Say something!"

"Me?" said Jonah.

"Who do you think?" said Toby. "Superman?"

"What was the question again?"

Mrs. Henderson looked at Jonah impatiently. "I asked what kind of atoms are in an atomic clock."

"Cesium atoms?" The answer popped out of his mouth before he had time to think.

"Correct. Bombarded by...?"

"Microwaves!" answered a girl wearing large, tortoise-shell glasses.

"That's correct, Amanda, but don't talk out."

"Yes, Mrs. Henderson."

"Follow me, class. We'll go inside the building." When they were all gathered together in the lobby, Mrs. Henderson looked at her wristwatch and pointed to a large clock on the wall. "Dr. Bailey should be here any minute. If you have a watch, you might want to check it against this one. After all, it's the most accurate clock in the world!"

I wonder what time it is on Grandpa Wiley's watch, but I don't dare look, Jonah thought.

"Mrs. Henderson?" asked Amanda.

"Yes?"

"Will we be able to touch the cesium?"

"We'll be able to *look* at it. Whether we'll be able to touch it, I really don't —"

"I can answer that question," said a man who was walking towards the group. He was tall and well built. *He looks more like a football player than a scientist.*

"Dr. Bailey?" said Mrs. Henderson.

"Yes. Glad to meet you," said Dr. Bailey, as he gave Mrs. Henderson a hearty handshake. He wore thick glasses and his hair was cut short. "You will *not* be allowed to touch cesium. It is a very volatile substance."

Amanda waved her hand in the air.

"Yes?" said Dr. Bailey.

"What does 'volatile' mean?"

"It means something that changes quickly. Cesium likes to bond to other atoms, especially oxygen. When it does, the result can be dangerous — fire or an explosion."

"Wow!" said Toby.

"We must handle it with extreme care," said Dr.

Bailey, glancing at Toby. "Before we begin our tour, I want to remind you of three rules: First, don't touch anything. Second, don't touch anything. Third, don't touch anything. Is that clear?"

"Yes, Dr. Bailey," answered a chorus of voices.

"Good. Follow me." He pressed a button and spoke into the intercom. A buzzer sounded and he pushed open the heavy door.

"This place is guarded like Fort Knox," said Toby.

"Shh!" said Mrs. Henderson, putting her index finger to her lips. They followed Dr. Bailey through the door, up one flight of stairs, and along a brightly lit hallway. They stopped outside a door with a sign saying AUTHORIZED PERSONNEL ONLY. Dr. Bailey opened the door.

"Here we are," said Dr. Bailey, pointing to a metallic tube. It was about twelve feet long and three feet in diameter. "We finished building our atomic clock only last year. We've nicknamed her 'Virginie'."

"But, sir, how is that a clock?" asked Deborah.

"Well, it's not the kind of clock you're familiar with. But anything is a clock if we can count something on a regular basis — like the back and forth movement of a pendulum, the unwinding of a spring, or the vibrations of a quartz crystal. The atomic clock is just a sophisticated way of counting how many times cesium atoms flip over."

"Sir? What's it ... I mean she, made of?" asked Amanda.

Dr. Bailey smiled. "She's made of aluminum plus other metals. Inside the tube, a small amount of cesium is being bombarded by microwaves. They cause the atoms to vibrate extremely fast. Does anyone know at what speed they vibrate?"

There was silence. Suddenly, a voice said, "9.2 billion rotations per second?" Everyone looked at Jonah in amazement. "I must have read it in a book," he mumbled, looking down at his feet.

"You're right, young man!" said Dr. Bailey. "Let me explain it this way. If the atomic clock had been set to run three million years ago, when humans first stood upright, the clock would not have gained or lost more than one second!"

The kids stared at Dr. Bailey. "Hard to imagine, isn't it? Especially when we realize that a few hundred years ago, people thought a clock was accurate even if it lost five minutes a day."

George Graham, Jonah thought. *I remember. That's what he said.*

Everyone walked around the tube that filled most of the room. Knobs and dials and gauges were placed at various spots on the tube.

"Look at me!" said Toby. He was making a face at his reflection in the tube. "I'm an alien from outer space!"

"Yeah, and so is your mother," said Deborah.

"Toby," snapped Mrs. Henderson. "Behave yourself."

"Children, come closer," said Dr. Bailey. "I want to show you something very special." Everyone crowded around Dr. Bailey. He unlocked a cupboard and brought out a small box. He opened the box and took out a tube the size of his index finger. A silver-gold-coloured metal shone with a strange lustre.

"Boys and girls, this is our Cesium-133. Beautiful, isn't it?" The children nodded their heads. "This one gram is enough to run our atomic clock for a year."

"Where does it come from?" asked Deborah.

"It's all around us, but hard to get."

"Sounds like a riddle," said Toby.

"You're right," said Dr. Bailey. "In some ways, science *is* like a riddle." He paused. "I suppose you've heard of granite?"

The children nodded.

"Well, granite is found everywhere in nature. From one cubic foot of granite we can extract one gram of cesium. Sounds easy, doesn't it?" The kids nodded. "But it's not. Although cesium can be extracted anywhere, it's very expensive to handle and package. Anyone know why?"

The hands shot up.

"Amanda?" said Dr. Bailey.

"Because it's so dangerous!" said Amanda.

"*And* can make you sick." Dr. Bailey put the tube carefully back into its box and placed the box on the counter behind him. "Follow me. There's something else I want to show you."

Everyone walked back down the hall, through a set of doors, down a flight of stairs, and into another room. A row of metal cabinets covered with dials and buttons and gauges were in the middle of the room. "Have you ever heard the National Research Council Time Signal on CBC radio?" Dr. Bailey asked.

"I have," said Amanda.

"Me too," said Deborah.

The girls looked at each other, giggled, and recited, "The beginning of the long dash following ten seconds of silence indicates exactly one p.m. Eastern Standard Time."

Dr. Bailey smiled. "Well done, girls!" He touched a cabinet. "We're the people who take care of that message. In fact," he added, "you might say we sell time."

"Sell time?" asked Elijah.

"His father is an accountant," whispered Deborah.

"Yes. What we sell is called a 'frequency standard'. We charge radio stations and even the new television stations for the absolute correct time. Banks, too. Can anyone tell me where else we might need accurate time?"

Silence. "I'll give you a clue. It's time that tells us where we are." There were more puzzled looks.

I remember, Jonah thought. *John Harrison said the same thing a long time ago.* "Navigation?"

"Right you are again," said Dr. Bailey. "Railways and airlines need to know the precise time." He pointed to Jonah. "I think that boy has the makings of a metrologist!"

"A weatherman?" said Amanda.

Dr. Bailey smiled. "That's a meteorologist. A metrologist is someone who measures things like weights and time."

"Oh," said Amanda, who didn't like to be wrong.

"Do you have any questions?" asked Dr. Bailey.

"Did you always want to be a ... metrologist?" asked Deborah.

Dr. Bailey shook his head. "Not really. I grew up on a farm in Saskatchewan. For a while, I was a high school teacher. In those days, I earned about $400 per year."

"How much do you make now?" asked Elijah.

"That, young man, is classified top secret," said Dr. Bailey, smiling at Elijah. "I eventually got my science degree. Soon after that, I moved here to work at the NRC."

Suddenly, Mrs. Henderson said, "Where's Toby?"

Jonah felt his heart skip a beat. *Have I lost Toby again?*

"The bathroom?" said Deborah.

"The bus?" said Elijah.

"Not without my permission," said Mrs. Henderson.

"Maybe one of the boys should go to the bathroom to look for him," said Dr. Bailey.

"I'll go," Jonah said quickly. "Um ... where is it?"

Dr. Bailey pointed towards his right.

Jonah hurried out of the room, down the hall, and into the boys' bathroom. "Toby?" he called. "You in here?"

He heard water dripping from a faucet. The white urinals were standing like ghostly sentinels against the wall.

"Toby?" he called again. He looked under the doors of the cubicles. Empty. Then, as he walked around the corner, he saw Toby. He was lying on the tile floor, crumpled in a heap.

"Toby? Are you okay?" Jonah shook his shoulder and turned him over.

Toby's face was pale. On the floor beside his hand was the small box that Dr. Bailey had left on the counter. Its cover was open and the tube was in Toby's hand. Very carefully, Jonah placed the tube back into the box.

"Toby?" No answer. Jonah's heart beat wildly. He went to the sink, turned on the tap, and splashed water on Toby's face. Toby didn't move. Then Jonah remembered about artificial respiration. He'd learned how to do it in swim class. *How do I do it again?*

He turned Toby over onto his stomach, got on top of him, and lifted Toby's arms. He pushed on his back, lifted his arms, pushed on his back. Over and over and over. Jonah's arms and shoulders were aching. The seconds seemed like minutes; the minutes seemed like hours.

Finally, Toby coughed and breathed in great gulps of air. "Wha … what's going on?"

Jonah collapsed on the floor beside Toby. "You stupid idiot! What were you trying to do?"

"I just wanted … to see … the cesium," Toby gasped.

"Do you have any idea how dangerous that was?"

Toby looked down on the ground. "Sorry. But I put the stopper back on when I started to feel sick."

"You were lucky."

"Are you going to tell on me?" The colour was coming back to Toby's face.

Jonah shook his head. "No, but that was sure a dumb thing to do!"

Toby nodded. "What should we do now?"

"We?"

"How do we put the cesium back?"

"Hold on there!"

"I'll owe you. Anything. Just name it."

Jonah put his arm around Toby's shoulders. "If we ever get out of here, if we ever get home, I want you to draw a picture of every place we've seen."

Toby grinned. "You've got it."

Jonah stood up. "Stay right here. I'll see if the coast is clear."

He walked out into the hall, looked both ways, and bumped right into a man. His hair was white and bushy. The smoke from his pipe wreathed around his head and rose to the ceiling. It was the Stranger! *I've got to talk to him, before he disappears again.*

"Mister?" said Jonah.

"Yes?" the man said, taking the pipe out of his mouth.

"I want … I *need* to talk to you."

The man raised his eyebrows and smiled at Jonah. "About what?"

"About time."

"Time?" asked the man. "I know a little about time. What is it you want to know?"

Jonah swallowed hard. "First of all, why or how, did you follow us?"

"That I do not know," the Stranger said. "One minute I was minding my own business when poof — I would see you. And poof! You were gone."

Jonah sighed. *All this time, I was sure the Stranger*

had the answers. And now it seems he knows as little as I do. "So you don't know how we can get home?"

"It is all relative, my boy," said the Stranger. "I will think about your problem." He drew his eyebrows together. "The watch, it allows you to travel through space and time?"

"Yes …"

"Then you must wind it one more time. You will be home." The man paused. "And boy?"

"Yes?"

"I would now like to go to the bathroom in peace and quiet."

Jonah followed the man back to the bathroom. "Thank you, Mr. …?"

"You do not know who I am?"

Jonah smiled. "Yes, now I think I do." He reached for Toby's hand. "Come on, Toby. We need to do something before we can go home."

"What are we waiting for?" Toby said. His hands were in his pockets and he whistled the "William Tell Overture" as they walked out of the bathroom.

"A good journey!" the Stranger called after them.

"And to you, too," answered Jonah.

They hurried back to the room where the cesium was stored. Jonah placed the box back on the counter. "Time now, Toby?"

"Let's get out of here!"

Jonah wound the watch. From far away, he could hear Mrs. Henderson's voice calling, "Jonah? Toby? Where are you?"

11

PRESENT TIME

The sun peeked through the window blinds and shone in Jonah's eyes. He touched the familiar softness of his quilt and snuggled into the warmth of his bed. Outside the window, he heard the twittering of birds, the thrum of car tires on the road, the shouts of kids playing in the street below.

He remembered everything — the places he had been, the people he had met, and the things he had done. He remembered a hot sun blazing in a clear sky, a quiet place of cold stone, and a lonely railway station near a river. He remembered a man telling stories, a woman peeling potatoes, and a gang of bullies beating him up.

Jonah took the chain off his neck and held the gold watch in the palm of his hand. The timepiece glowed in the early morning light. *I can't change things that happened in the past. Mom and Dad are divorced. Dad has remarried. But maybe something good can come from something bad.*

Jonah knew what he had to do. Climbing out of bed, he put on his bathrobe and walked down the stairs. He found his father sitting at the kitchen table.

"Dad, can I talk to you?"

"Sure," said Mr. Wiley, putting down his newspaper. "Where is everyone?"

"Pam took Toby for his art lesson." Mr. Wiley paused. "Toby said he had some drawings he wanted to get started on."

Jonah put his hand in his pocket and pulled out the watch. "Dad, I need to give this back to you."

"Grandpa Wiley's watch?" Mr. Wiley frowned. "But … what are you doing with it?"

Jonah swallowed hard. "I … I took it."

Mr. Wiley stared at Jonah. "You *took* it?"

"I didn't *mean* to take it. It just sort of …"

"What?"

Jonah shook his head. "You wouldn't believe me."

"I might," Mr. Wiley said softly. "Tell me."

"You'll think I'm crazy if I tell you."

"I promise you that I won't."

Jonah sat down on the chair opposite his father. "Well … I felt … it was pulling me to take it."

Mr. Wiley nodded.

"I want to tell you what happened, but I don't know where to start."

"At the beginning is always a good place," said Mr. Wiley.

Jonah took a big breath. "I don't know how it happened. When I wound the watch, I went to other places and to other times."

Mr. Wiley smiled. He had a faraway look in his eyes.

"Dad?"

"The truth is," Mr. Wiley said, "the same thing happened to me when I was about your age."

Jonah let out his breath. Up until that moment, he wasn't sure if he had dreamed the whole thing or if he was crazy or if everything that had happened had been real.

"And you came back?" Jonah said.

"As you see."

"And now?"

"Now it's time …" Mr. Wiley hesitated.

"Yes?"

"It's time … for me to give the watch to you."

"You're letting me *keep* it?"

"It's not mine to give. You see, son, the watch can never be owned. It must be passed on from one generation to the next. Grandpa Wiley explained that to me a long time ago. And when it's time, you'll give it to your son or your daughter."

Jonah nodded. "I will, Dad. I promise."

Jonah's fingers closed over the warmth of the watch.

"Dad?"

"Yes?"

"I'm glad I'm home."

ACKNOWLEDGEMENTS

The author would like to thank the following individuals for their valuable contributions to this novel:

William J. H. Andrewes, Curator of exhibit, *The Art of the Timekeeper*. The Frick Collection, New York City.

Chris Bailey, Curator, American Clock & Watch Museum, Bristol, Connecticut.

Sylvie Bertrand, Librarian, Canada Science and Technology Museum, Ottawa.

Beth N. Bisbano, Director/Archivist, The National Watch & Clock Museum, Columbia, Pennsylvania.

Dr. Jean-Simon Boulanger, Group Leader, Frequency & Time, Institute of National Measurement Standards, National Research Council of Canada, Ottawa.

Dr. Randall Brooks, Curator, Physical Sciences & Space, Canada Science and Technology Museum, Ottawa.

Sheila Freedman, Librarian, Barbara Frum Branch, Toronto Public Library, Toronto.

Sharon Gordon, Librarian, The National Watch & Clock Museum, Columbia, Pennsylvania.

Julie Kirsh, Director, Electronic Information, *Toronto Sun*, Toronto.

Sharon McCleave, Professor, Human Biology, School of Health Sciences, Seneca College of Applied Arts and Technology, Toronto.

Dr. Hooley McLaughlin, Senior Advisor for Science & Technology, Ontario Science Centre, Toronto.

Catherine Rondina, Librarian, North York Central Branch, Toronto Public Library, Toronto.

Mirjana Sebek-Heroldova, Manager, Czech Tourist Authority, Toronto.

Alexandra Shaw, Institute of National Measurement Standards, National Research Council of Canada, Ottawa.

Beverley Spencer, Librarian, North York Central Branch, Toronto Public Library, Toronto.

Kevin von Appen, Associate Director, Digital Media and Publications, Ontario Science Centre, Toronto.

Fellow writers: Ronnie Arato, Barbara Greenwood, Mark Mazer, Judy Nisenholt, Rivanne Sandler, Tom Sankey, Judy Saul, Liliane Schacter, Muriel Tinianov, Sydell Waxman, Lynn Westerhout, Frieda Wishinsky.

And others who helped along the way: Meryl Arbing, Barbara Berson, Miriam Dryer, Max and Julia Dublin, John Freund, Carmen Horvath and her son, Emil, Phyllis Rose, Dr. Alvin Sher, Bev Sidney, Linda R. Silver, Sheila Smolkin, Sheryn Weber.

The creative, committed people at Dundurn Press: Margaret Bryant, Michael Carroll, Laura Harris, Courtney Horner, Karen McMullin, and Diane Young.

GLOSSARY

armillary sphere: Model of Ptolemy's universe with Earth in the centre, made up of bands showing the celestial equator, tropics, ecliptic, etc.

celestial: Pertaining to the sky or the heavens.

cesium: A white, ductile element of the alkali metal group. It is the most electropositive element and has photoelectric properties.

chronometer: Traditionally a timekeeper with a detent escapement, but used by the Swiss for watches with special timekeeping certificates issued by an official rating bureau.

clepsydra: Greek name for water clock.

clock: A device, other than a watch, for measuring and indicating time, based on some strictly periodic process (e.g. the swing of a pendulum, the vibration of a crystal, the diurnal rotation of the earth about its axis) whose period is regarded as constant.

clockmaker: A maker, or repairer, of clocks.

clockwork: The mechanism of a clock.

dial: A circle around or on which a scale is marked, so that the position of one or more pointers, rotating about the centre of the circle, can be stated.

escapement: The part of a clock linking the oscillator (balance or pendulum) to the power source (spring or weight) and controlling the rate.

foliot: An oscillating bar with a weight at each end, used in the first mechanical timekeepers as a controller.

fusée: The trumpet-shaped pulley used in earlier spring-driven timepieces with a gut line or chain to provide an even power drive.

gear: A device for connecting the moving parts of a machine, usually by the engagement of toothed wheels or their equivalent, so that the speed of rotation of one part causes a different speed of rotation of the other part.

grasshopper escapement: An ingenious escapement that needed no oiling, devised by John Harrison.

lathe: A machine used to shape or cut wood, metal etc. which holds the material fast in rapid rotation against the cutting component.

longitude: The angular distance between the meridian passing through a given point on the Earth's surface and the poles, and the standard meridian at Greenwich, England. It is measured in degrees east or west of Greenwich, which represents 0 degrees longitude.

metrology: The science of weights and measures.

pendulum: An oscillator that depends on its length and the force of gravity.

quadrant: An instrument with a calibrated arc of 90 degrees, used for measuring angles and formerly, before the sextant was developed, for measuring altitudes.

sandglass: Interval timer depending on the flow of sand from one chamber to another.

shaft: A long, smooth-surfaced piece of wood or metal of roughly the same thickness throughout its length and usually of roughly circular cross section.

sundial: A device which during hours of sunlight indicates the time by a shadow cast by a stationary arm (gnomon) on a dial marked in hours.

time: The physical quantity measured by clocks.

verge escapement: The earliest and most persistent escapement, comprising a staff (the verge) with balance and pallets, and a crown wheel.

watch: A small portable timepiece worked by a coiled spring, and designed to be worn on the wrist or carried in a pocket.

watchmaker: A person who makes or repairs watches.

Definitions are from *The History of Clocks & Watches* by Eric Bruton. (London: Little, Brown & Company, 1999), and *The New Lexicon Webster's Encyclopedic Dictionary of the English Language* (Canadian Edition, 1988).

AUTHOR'S NOTE

The verse in chapter four was composed by Anonymous, excerpted from *The Jade Flute: Chinese Poems in Prose* (White Plains, NY: Peter Pauper Press, 1960), 5. Used with permission.

The verse contained in chapter five was composed by Bernard of Cluny, ca. 1145; translated by John Mason Neale, 1851. *Medieval Hymns and Sequences,* Third Edition. (London: Joseph Masters, 1867).

The quotation that appears in chapter ten is the National Research Council Time Signal and heard in Canada on CBC Radio. It is the longest-running radio announcement in Canadian radio history, and was first heard on November 5, 1939. (National Research Council Canada. "Frequently Asked Questions". http://www.nrc-cnrc.gc.ca/eng/services/time/).